INTO THE NIGHT WITH A STRANGER

To Sue
with grateful thanks
for your support

Joan

INTO THE NIGHT WITH A STRANGER

Joan Khurody

© Joan Khurody, 2016

Published by Joan Khurody

A CIP catalogue record for this book is available from the British Library.

ISBN 978-0-9932558-3-0

Book layout by Clare Brayshaw

Prepared and printed by:

York Publishing Services Ltd

64 Hallfield Road
Layerthorpe
York YO31 7ZQ

Tel: 01904 431213

Website: www.yps-publishing.co.uk

ONE

The car pulled into the drive just before midday. Ann watched the driver get out, adjust her skirt and stare curiously round her. It had to be Jess but it was hard to take this in. The rather plump and somewhat crumpled woman outside seemed a complete stranger. Then they were face to face at the door and she met the familiar, bright blue gaze. Her breath caught in her throat and she could not manage a word of greeting but Jess, ignoring any awkwardness, enveloped them both in a concealing cloud of talk about her journey, as if nothing had changed, as if they had never parted.

"Ann! At last! I'm exhausted. It's taken me over three hours to get here. There just isn't any direct route from Oxford to Norfolk, but it was the last few miles that I found really complicated. You certainly are off the beaten track and your country roads are *so* confusing. Incredibly narrow and winding! I got lost twice. I have absolutely no sense of direction."

"You usually get where you want to be in the end though." Ann's voice was dry and her face expressionless. "You'd better come in."

Jess shot her a wary glance. "I've left my things in the boot. I'll just get them."

Returning with a small suitcase and two carrier bags, she followed Ann into a cool, square hall that smelled faintly of leather and lavender.

"What shall I do with these? There's wine and some delicious chocolates. I'm glad that I didn't bring flowers. You already have a gorgeous display on that table over there. It reminds me of the hours I used to spend on arrangements like that. Do you remember?"

Ann was gripped by a fierce indignation. How dare Jess speak of the past so casually? How dare she call on memory so openly?

"Put everything down there," she said tightly, "and we'll deal with it all after we've had a drink. Come through here."

She led the way into a large conservatory where decanters and glasses, set out on a silver tray, stood ready on a painted sideboard.

"A gin? A sherry?"

"Sherry would be lovely." Jess went over to the window. "This place isn't at all as I imagined it. You always talked about the cottage and I pictured it as small and cosy but the house is really large and the garden seems huge." Her voice wavered a little. "It's a lot to have to look after on your own."

Handing her a glass, Ann went back to the tray to get something for herself and bent over it without speaking. Jess drew an audible breath.

"It was terrible when I heard about your mother. She was *so* strong. I found it hard to believe that you had lost her. I kept thinking of you. I longed to see you. It was *so* dreadful......." She faltered into silence, Ann's grim, unresponsive face bringing her sharply up against all that lay bitter and broken between them.

They had met in Bombay in 1966, both in their early twenties, both newly married and living abroad for the first time and both still somewhat overwhelmed by the city's steamy, chaotic vibrancy. Their friendship had been instantaneous and intense. It had ended badly. They had been very close for five years but hadn't seen each other for almost ten and, unexpectedly together again, were now edging their way along a precipice of potential distress and disappointment, unsure of what exactly they hoped for from this meeting.

"Ann," Jess was shaky but determined, "there are too many things it's impossible to say but I can't be here and not speak about your parents. I never met your father but I always understood how difficult it was for you when he died so unexpectedly, and you know how fond I became of your mother when she came out to stay with you in India after his death. Now she too…." She ran a finger round the rim of her glass. "It must help with …" she paused, "…with everything that you still have this lovely family home."

Ann took several slow sips from her drink, caught, despite herself, by this evocative phrase and the images it aroused; images of a time before discord and disaster; a time when such things were unimaginable; a time before she had met an outsider and gone off to a foreign country with him; a time when everything around her had seemed to be soothingly familiar and set to last forever. How carelessly she had accepted, and how casually rejected, that tranquil life. Her parents had been undemonstrative country people, not given to extravagant gestures, but she could never shake off the irrational feeling that their early deaths had been a final, stark repudiation of the choice that she had made.

She pulled herself back to the present. Normal conversation might be difficult, unsustainable even, but she had to make an effort. She went over to join Jess who had moved to the doorway and was standing there, holding her sherry and looking out into the sunlit garden.

"You're right. Being here does help. I am lucky that I still owned the place when I finally came back to England. I could have sold up when Mother died. That would have been the rational thing to do. The garden was a bit neglected even then and, in the years that I stayed on in India and the place was rented out, none of the tenants did much to it. It was a jungle when I came home and took it in hand three years ago."

"Could we go out and explore it?"

Ann nodded and they set down their glasses and stepped out into the sunshine, crossing a paved terrace and following a curved path that led away from the house through beds of lavender and roses, loud with bees and shimmering with butterflies.

"It's a heavenly garden. You must spend all your time in it."

"I'm not a complete rural recluse," snapped Ann, adding in a softer tone, "I do work hard in it and I give my plants lots of TLC."

"That sounds rather like the violent antiseptic your mother used to dispense around Bombay in such quantities. As if she were trying to sanitise India single-handedly."

"TCP, you mean. For my mother that was much the same thing. No! That's wildly unfair. She belonged to a generation that dealt in practical ways with every kind of hurt."

For the first time their eyes met and held, Ann's steady but opaque, projecting a weight of unvoiced pain into the

4

space between them. Then, with an impatient shake of her head, she turned away and they walked on in silence across a wide lawn until they reached an archway in a high, perfectly trimmed hedge at the far side of it. Jess stopped abruptly and breathing in the scent of a honeysuckle that hung heavily above them, plucked a spray of blossom and crushed it between her fingers.

"It's lovely here. Why on earth did you take so long to come back?"

Ann rounded on her. "Take care, Jess. So far we've avoided dangerous topics. Talking about my parents was a delaying tactic. It isn't them we are thinking about. We both know that we are only postponing what we need to say to each other; that we both dread having to face up to it. When you wrote asking if we could meet, I found that very tough to deal with."

The unwelcome letter had arrived two weeks earlier, announcing that Jess was on a visit to England, spending several weeks with her parents, but any news it contained had been incidental. Essentially it had been a plea for reconciliation. This had seemed impossible. Anger was a potent analgesic that Ann had held on to throughout their long estrangement and she had been shaken by this reminder of just how raw the scars left by tragedy and betrayal still were. She had told herself that she was living another life – had indeed lived two lives – since they last saw each other and that it was madness to go back over all that past heartache. Yet their parting had been so out of her control that she had never completely suppressed a lingering need for confrontation, for resolution, and, against all the odds, she had dashed off a reply, suggesting that Jess should come for this weekend.

Straightening her shoulders, she said, "I had never expected to hear from you again. It was a shock. You reminded me that we hadn't met for over nine years and I resented your implication. You seemed to be setting some sort of statute of limitation. Well, in spite of everything, I agreed to see you. You've come. You........No......I have to....... Look, there are some chairs over there. You stay out here for a while. I'll go and get lunch. I'll call you when it's ready. We can't carry on like this. We do have to talk. We'll talk then."

Without waiting for a response she strode off and re-entered the house. Collecting the suitcase from the hall, she took it up to a pretty back bedroom where, still holding it, she went to the window and saw that Jess was sitting on the lawn with her arms wrapped around herself, uncharacteristically forlorn. She turned back into the room. Like all the others in the cottage, it was much used but inviting, its well-worn furniture polished and gleaming. She had taken extra care when preparing it for this visit, adding a new patchwork quilt and setting a good selection of books, a box of biscuits and a vase of highly scented roses on the bedside table. She felt a stab of annoyance at this evidence of her weakness and thumping the suitcase onto the floor, went back downstairs where she snatched up the wine and the chocolates and took them through into the kitchen. Moving briskly around, assembling the cold meats and salads that she had partially prepared earlier that morning, she slapped things onto plates, immersed in a furious, internal monologue.

"Why did I let her come? Well, I'll just have to get through these two days. Then she'll go and I can get on with my life. How does she find the nerve to ask impossible questions? Why *did* I take so long to come back? Somehow, after....

after it all happened, staying on in Bombay seemed the right thing, the *only* thing, to do but was I simply holding on to my pride, denying people the 'I told you so' routine, or did I believe that I was working my passage back to my old self, my old life? Is that what this really is? I thought I was coming home but once you step outside the boundaries and ignore the rules, you find that you are never completely at home wherever you are."

She came to a halt, unaware of the large dish that she was holding and it suddenly tilted, its contents spilling over the floor. Kneeling down to clear the mess, she brushed away a few sticky tears. The food was ruined and had to be thrown in the bin and she banged the empty container down roughly on the table.

"Self-pity won't help. What happened was almost unbearable and it wasn't easy to carry on but there were people in India who cared for me. How could I have let that frighten me? When it came to making choices again, I panicked. Let's face it. In the end, I came back here through sheer cowardice. It was a one woman stampede. I trampled over everyone. I behaved very badly."

Though the day was warm and she was sweating slightly from her efforts, a shiver ran through her. She sat down and rested her arms on the scrubbed oak table. The homeliness of this kitchen usually steadied and consoled her. Even though her reoccupation of it had been difficult and, entering it, she frequently half expected to see her mother at the stove and her father standing near the window, she had slowly been making her peace with these gentle ghosts. Why had she allowed that other sorrow to invade what she was fashioning into a sanctuary? With a deep sigh, she rose, picked up the tray that she had filled almost automatically and carried it out onto the terrace, where a table was already laid with a white cloth, floral plates and a posy in a delicate vase. She was grateful that it was a sunny day and they could eat outside. The garden was a comforting place in times of stress. She stood taking in the scene that she had created, waiting for the breeze and the scent of flowers to soothe her. On these bright days, she usually found herself relaxing into old, unthinking ways. But the spell was broken. Jess had opened a door into the past that she had been struggling to keep closed. She drew a calming breath and called out, "Lunch is ready."

"How pretty that is, Ann. Really. It's quite idyllic." Jess, coming up from the garden, was holding on to the air of normality that she had been trying for since her arrival.

"We don't seem to have been cut out for idylls though, do we?" Ann's voice was harsh.

Jess sat down heavily at the table, her head bent. For several minutes she did not move or speak and Ann, who had taken a seat opposite her and been aimlessly shifting her cutlery around, banged her knife down beside her plate.

"I said that we would talk over lunch, Jess. You know that we have to."

Jess straightened in her seat and looked up at her. The clear, perfect outline of her small face had blurred and lost its definition and her once glossy bob had faded, as if misted with fine rain, but her blue eyes were as compelling as ever.

"Do you hate me Ann?"

"I don't know. Hearing from you, seeing you, has made old feelings flare up. I've tried to forget it all and living in this place is an antidote to tragedy and drama, but what happened hasn't ever ceased to hurt and it's still unfinished business.

8

We were torn apart by events. It was a very unsatisfactory ending."

Again they sat for several, fraught minutes, caught up in thoughts of the past. Then Ann leaned forward, her face white and tense.

"What happened that night? That morning?"

TWO

As she entered the stuffy chaos of the college room, Ann was instantly aware of a young man standing somewhat apart from the daunting crowd of boisterous students in front of her. His eyes were deep lidded and fringed with incredibly long lashes and his dark brows met over a strong, straight nose. Many English faces are blobs of impressionistic paint. You create them for yourself. This face was a line drawing. It already existed with an incisive clarity.

The friendly girl who had impulsively invited her to the party, came over with a cheerful greeting and, noticing where her eyes lingered, took her hand and led her across the room.

"Meet Sam Mehta. He's from India. A Parsi, if you know what that is. But he's a darling. Sam, this is Ann Baker. Look after her for me." Smiling rather distractedly at them, she dashed away to greet someone else.

No-one could have foreseen any connection between Ann and Sam. There was every kind of distance between them. She had grown up in rural England, within an insular but robust and self-confident farming community and he belonged to a predominantly urban and sophisticated Indian minority that over many generations had held on to a distinct but increasingly fragile identity. She had been born in an English market town, in a cottage hospital set in lush, green gardens and he within the dusty, desert precincts of a palace in Rajasthan, where his grandfather was one of the Maharaja's officials and where his mother, following an old custom, had been staying with her parents for the birth of her first child. There was quiet satisfaction over Ann's arrival but little fuss. Sam had caused considerably greater excitement. Celebratory gifts of traditional sweets in gold foil boxes were sent out to friends and relatives. An elaborate horoscope had been cast, and preserved in the form of a leather-bound booklet of complex, beautifully drawn astrological charts accompanied by an explanatory text. This, though it did predict many of the key dates and events of his life, had not, in fact, mentioned 1964. Yet, here he was, in October of that year, being introduced to Ann.

"Hello, Ann. *Do* you know what a Parsi is?"

"I must admit that I don't."

"Then I must set you right from the start. I don't want you thinking that I am something weird. I'm definitely not a fire worshipper."

This sounded to Ann as if it might be a smoothly rehearsed line but she had no idea what he was talking about and he saw her bewilderment.

"Don't worry. I'll tell you all about it somewhere and sometime less noisy. It's impossible to really talk in this racket. Let's go and get something to drink."

She was quite happy to go to the makeshift bar and then move round the crowded room with him and, although he had appeared aloof at first sight, he knew most of the people there and seemed so at ease with them that she too relaxed and found herself enjoying the evening. Then, after about an hour, he took her hand.

"Look, I would like to be able to have a proper conversation. It's still surprisingly warm outside and there's a moon, so it's not that dark. You must know Parker's Piece, the green just down the road. We could walk around there and be able to hear each other speak."

She looked directly at him. This was not her natural environment. It was the first of such parties for her and she had only recently emerged from a very staid world in which one simply did not walk out into the night with a stranger. He was caught by her gaze and her hesitation. For several seconds they stared at each other and it seemed that whatever they drew from this long look reassured both of them. Ann slowly nodded and they went out together and walked the short distance to the large green that he had mentioned. There was still a scattering of people about, some, seduced by the exceptional mildness, even sitting in groups on the grass and, while at first neither of them seemed to actually want to talk, content after the noise of the party to stroll around and simply enjoy one another's presence, they too finally found a quiet spot and sat down.

"I've gathered that you aren't a student," Sam said. "Do your family belong to Cambridge?"

"No. They live outside a small market town in Norfolk. About fifty miles from here. My father owns a bookshop there."

"Why are you in Cambridge then?"

"Well, my father wants me to work in the shop with him but he felt that I should have some outside experience first. I did a secretarial course in Norwich after I left school and then he arranged for me to come here. One of his friends has a bookshop. In the centre. I'm working there. That's how I know so many students."

"Where do you live while you're here?"

"I have a room in the house of my father's friend's friend. My parents do want me to have some freedom but they're not taking too many chances."

Sam shot a penetrating glance at her. "Would *you* like to take chances?"

His tone startled her into self-revelation. "When I first came here I was very homesick. It made me feel that freedom might be rather lonely. I'm used to being safe and not having to make decisions but I do sometimes wish I could be more adventurous."

"Do you have any brothers or sisters?"

"No. I'm an only child. Do you have a large family?"

Sam smiled. "I expect you have a picture of India's teeming millions. Sorry! I was only teasing. I have just one brother, Cyrus. He's studying Medicine in London."

"What's your subject, Sam?"

"Economics. This is my final year. I'll be going home in the summer.

"Where is home exactly?"

"Bombay. Many Parsis live there. Look! I didn't bring you out here for a history lesson but it's probably a good idea to get this over and done with. If people don't know exactly what I am, it can make life difficult. Basically, my ancestors lived in Persia and followed the teachings of a prophet called Zoroaster. Because they always keep a sacred fire burning in their temples, they are often wrongly described as fire worshippers, but Zoroastrianism is far more complex than that. It was once the state religion of a great empire. Then, over a thousand years ago, Moslems became the rulers in Persia and many Zoroastrians fled to India. They became known as Parsis. An Indianised form of Persians."

"It sounds very exotic."

"No!" Sam was almost shouting. "That's our history. Our lives are like yours. Ordinary. It's a different history and setting but it's just a life."

They were both shaken by his outburst and sat quietly for a while looking out across the shadowy green.

"Is it lonely for you here, Sam?"

He turned to her but didn't answer. Their faces were very close. Ann could feel his warm breath. She had a sensation of her whole being dissolving in her tingling lips and she wanted to touch them to Sam's taut cheek. He put his hand over hers for a second and then withdrew it and looked away.

"I'm used to being lonely. I was often lonely at home. That isn't the problem. It's difficult to describe. It would be simplistic and trite to say that I feel misunderstood." He turned back towards her. "It's just that, occasionally, someone will explain something to me, speaking very kindly and slowly and, seeing how they think of me, I become a stranger to myself, as if what I am is undefined and ambiguous. In India all the very diverse elements that construct Sam Mehta are tacitly understood and that kind of understanding makes you real to yourself. You can't tell people that while you belong to a unique and ancient culture of which they are totally unaware, you have always had access to theirs; that you went to a school run by English masters; that your father has travelled all over the world; that you love Western music and mostly speak English within a tri-lingual family. You just smile and close down."

"I'm sorry if I made you feel like that."

"I'm sorry that I shouted at you."

Again they sat for some time without speaking, silenced by the dangerous possibilities of words. By now people were drifting away. Clouds were obscuring the moon and it grew darker and colder. They would soon be alone, islanded in the wide stretch of slightly damp grass, buffeted by an increasingly strong breeze.

"We'll have to go." Ann sounded reluctant. "It is getting very chilly."

They stood up and walked slowly to the small side road where she lodged. As they turned into it, Sam said, "Because my father has high expectations of me and people here aren't always sure what to think of me, I'm very careful about everything that I say and do but, though we've only spent a short time together, it's as if something in me has unclenched. I feel so relaxed with you, Ann." They had reached her front door. "I'm glad we've met. Can I see you again? Soon? Tomorrow?"

The following evening, they met in a small restaurant that Sam liked and as they sat down at their table, Ann smiled a little tremulously. "It's nice to share a proper meal with someone. I didn't appreciate how important that is till now. I took it for granted. We have a very old-fashioned, formal dining room at home and my mother is a stickler for a well laid table. It's been a bit bleak heating up tins of stew and beans on an electric ring and eating alone, no frills, no conversation and a less than varied menu."

"How long have you been doing that?"

"Just over three months and I haven't been home at all. My father is adamant that I should see what it is like to cope on my own. It's quite funny really. He's very much in charge of everything. Even my independence! He couldn't resist coming to see me after my first week here but he's kept strictly to the rules – his rules – since then."

"That sounds like my father. In our family we are used to him managing all our affairs. Both my brother and I are finding being away from him very liberating. We still have to report to headquarters in writing but that gives us much more leeway."

Their dawning realisation of what it meant to be the child of a controlling father was an immediate bond. They recognised in each other an isolating seriousness fostered by an over-protected, over-managed childhood. Sam, whatever he said, was accustomed to, and accepting of, his father's rigorous surveillance and Ann had always discussed everything with her parents – a simple and straightforward life having made this easy. Neither had ever contemplated rebellion but, together, they grew increasingly conscious of such a dangerous and heady possibility.

Sam was happier and more contented than ever before. His childhood had been an emotionally arid affair. His father, a driven, self-made success, had seen the imposition of discipline as the essential duty of a parent and had forcefully insisted on this to his wife. "Whatever you do, don't fuss over the boys. They will need to be tough to make their way in the world. We don't want to weaken them with any pampering." Occasionally, when he was very young, Sam had flung himself on his father in an attempted hug, only to see him straightening his tie and brushing down his lapels as if something distasteful had happened. Vague memories of sitting on his mother's lap with her arms around him were overlaid with images of a succession of ayahs. These women, though carefully instructed by his parents, had been irrepressibly volatile and easily moved, but as easily moved to anger as affection. He had certainly received many surreptitious slaps when they were alone with him. Then, at the age of eleven, he was sent to boarding-school where he became increasingly shut in on himself. Ann more than fulfilled a longstanding need. Her shy but obvious admiration of him and their undemanding companionship with its sensual undercurrents at last gave him the courage to abandon his defensive attitude and to emerge from a chilly self-sufficiency into shared and nourishing warmth.

Ann's feelings were rather more confused. The people she lived amongst, shaped by the seasonal round of down-to-earth tasks involved in growing crops and caring for livestock, were restrained in manner and laconic in speech. They were not in the habit of talking about their feelings or speculating about those of other people and had no time for what they described as idle chatter. Matter-of-fact conversation and gentle kisses were the reality of love as she had seen it play out around her. Introduced to books at an early age by her father, she was exceptionally well-read and aware of the more desperate loves of fiction, but all the measured voices of her childhood cast doubt on the validity of such excesses. Now, experiencing her own desperate moments and occasionally shaken by frighteningly intense needs, she found those same internalised voices urging caution.

At a deep level, they were both conscious of a capacity for passionate feeling but their backgrounds and upbringing had suppressed any easy spontaneity in them and they felt a hesitancy, a need to go slowly. Almost without conscious thought, they chose to spend much of their time together in public places and yet, for the next eight months, they essentially shared a private world that was totally hidden from the people who had always directed their lives so carefully. They were fully aware of the hazards of their growing intimacy and this awareness led them into a prolonged period of secrecy, an unusual lack of openness.

One evening in late May, Sam took Ann to a classical concert that he had been very much looking forward to. He had regularly been to such performances but it was a first for her and, as she looked round the rather drab hall and settled into a hard and uninviting chair, she found Sam's enthusiasm difficult to understand. Then the conductor raised his baton, the musicians became a single focused entity producing heart-stopping music and, moved and exhilarated, she, like the players, folded herself around this. She had always enjoyed the light melodies available at home and school but this was a revelation and opened up something in her that her prosaic upbringing had completely suppressed. She barely registered the formalities at the end of the performance and came out of the hall in a daze, clutching Sam's arm in a way that made him glance around them. He was wary of public display and nervous of public disapproval. Nothing had been openly discussed but he had always supposed that Ann was driven by similar anxieties.

"A drink? A coffee, Ann? Where shall we go?"

"I don't want anything. Everywhere will be so noisy and I can still hear those glorious sounds. I just want.......I think I'd better go home."

Glancing at her intense, closed expression, Sam did not attempt to speak as they walked slowly back to her lodging. Though they knew that the elderly couple who owned the house always went to bed at ten, an ingrained caution had always led them to part at the gate without any fuss but, that evening, Ann took his hand and led him round to a small gazebo in the back garden. And suddenly they were in each other's arms, lost in kisses that bore no resemblance to their earlier polite embraces. A light went on in the bathroom above and Ann froze. Even after months of discretion and secrecy and her failure to say anything about Sam to her family, she knew that there was nothing shameful between them but she could never totally overcome the discomfort of someone conditioned to conformity and accustomed to approbation.

"I'm sorry Sam. I'm sorry."

"There's nothing to be sorry about. We both know how it is. Don't worry. We'll find our way. I love you, Ann."

The light above went out and they moved closer. It was the first time that love had been spoken of. They kissed again, a long, slow, body-melting fusion of lips and then rested breathlessly against each other for a moment before Ann put her palm against Sam's cheek and drew away. They walked quietly round to the front door, not even holding hands.

Later that week, after they had ordered an evening meal in their usual restaurant, Sam drew out a letter.

"I've just had this from my father. He's full of plans for me. He's looking to set up all sorts of contacts for me in Bombay during August."

"Well it's what you expected. We've tried to ignore it but we always knew that you would have to be back by then."

"Ann, what are we going to do? You're right. We have been avoiding this discussion. There just seemed to be so many probable complications and difficulties ahead of us that it was easier not to think about them. We've been behaving as if this part of our life would go on forever, shutting our eyes to hard facts. We have to face up to them."

"Are you saying this is the end?"

"That's just not possible. You know how I feel. I love you. But how can I expect you to come to India with me. You'd have to leave so much behind and I can't begin to describe what it would be like for you there. You told me that you found Cambridge noisy and crowded at first. You really haven't any idea what those words can mean. Apart from the sheer din of everyday activities, you would be plunged into an ongoing operatic drama. You are used to people who live very private lives and never flaunt their feelings but the people you'd have to live with are in the habit of flaunting theirs all over the place. Just describing it all makes me feel how impossible it is to ask you to face it. I think that even I will find it hard to readjust. I may not be totally at home here but will I ever again be totally at home there? It's not easy to move between two worlds, Ann,"

She leaned towards him, her mouth quivering, and put her hand over his. She forgot all her usual caution and was totally unaware of anyone around them.

"I want to come. I will come."

"Ann! You'll marry me!"

"That's what I suppose you have in mind, Sam. Our parents may be dismayed by that idea but any other arrangement would hardly thrill them."

"How can you be so cool? Let's go. I have to be somewhere to hold you close."

"Sam. Be sensible. We've already ordered. We have to eat. More importantly, we have to talk. We both know how it will be. This will be hard for our families. They will all be upset and disappointed in their different ways and we've only made things worse by not saying anything about each other before this." She looked anxiously at him, struck by a strong feeling that they must not allow themselves to be separated or they might lose their courage and it would all be over. "What do you plan to do? I'm sure that it wouldn't work if you were to go home alone and I followed you later. So much could go wrong. I think I should travel with you and there isn't that much time before you leave. That means we have real problems."

"That means that I must write home. My father has to be told about us immediately."

"At least you can write. I'll have to break the news face to face. I know that both my mother and my father only want me to be happy but it will be a blow for them. All their plans for me will be changed and they aren't used to change."

She arranged to take two days off work and sent a note to her parents, saying that she would be home the following week because she had something important to discuss. She was quite sure about what she was doing but was eager to talk over with them such concerns as she did have. Sam, too, had concerns that he had not confided to Ann. He had not told her how deeply a sense of a special and separate destiny ran in his community and how what he was doing might be seen at some level as a betrayal, and he knew how much he was still dependent on, and tied to, his father. He spent hours on a series of draft letters that were all irritably discarded. Only after deciding that he must be simple and direct, did he finally manage to complete and post a version that he found acceptable.

THREE

Jessica Mason struck many people as light-weight and frivolous but this was largely because many people equate light-heartedness with light-mindedness and make lazy assumptions about petite, pretty females. She was an intelligent girl. Her parents, dedicated teachers, had carefully monitored her progress through her High School in Oxford and were satisfied with the respectable degree in English literature that she had gained from her redbrick university. Though this was far from prescriptive, being more an indicator of ability than a qualification for anything specific, they expected her to find rewarding work of some kind. They wanted her to take time to explore all the possible avenues open to her and straightforwardly offered her a holiday period before her search began.

Jess regarded them fondly as they discussed all this with her. She had not found school or college particularly demanding and was glad to have made them happy but she knew that she was about to disappoint them. Their strongly expressed views on equality and their fervent advocacy of genuine careers for women were constant background themes that had echoed throughout her life but made little impact on her. Her mother and father, usually so rational and cerebral, had married late and been rocked to the core when she was born, finding themselves at the mercy of deeper feelings than they had ever known. Their overwhelming pride in her had imbued her with a bone-deep conviction of her own worth and an unshakeable belief that she was equal to anyone and anything. She felt no compulsion to prove herself and deplored the stress that her graduate friends were under in scrambling for prestigious and well-paid jobs. She took a long, cool look at the future. What, in the end, would be gained from so much effort? Life was short and the sensible thing to do was to enjoy it. Her best course was to marry as soon as possible and to marry someone well-established in a career of his own, who could take over her parents' task of looking after the basics of existence, leaving her free to do just that.

"Are you at home for supper tomorrow?" her father asked at breakfast, one morning. "I've been introduced to a young man from the High Commission in India who has just arrived on leave from Bombay. He's agreed to talk to my sixth form boys about the country and his work there and I've invited him to join us. It would be nice for him to have your company too."

Jess, frequently out these days, was expected at a party the following evening but this guest sounded intriguing. She decided to make her excuses in order to meet him and the minute that he walked into their sitting room she saw that he might be the kind of eligible man that she was looking for. And he was a man. Most of her many admirers were still unacceptably boyish. It was not only their uncertain status that was against them. They were often decidedly puppyish and over-eager in their approaches to her. They were fun but they were not what she was looking for.

"Jess, this is Bob Clark. Bob, meet my daughter, Jess. I'll leave you to get to know each other while I see what my wife is up to in the kitchen and tell her that you've arrived. We'll be with you in a minute."

As her father went out of the room, Jess turned to Bob. She had to look up at him. He was very tall. He wasn't particularly good-looking but she liked what she saw. He was strong and athletic in build, with short, sandy hair, serious hazel eyes and a square, firm-jawed face.

"Did your talk go well? I'm sure the boys enjoyed it. Everyone is so fascinated by India. It seems such an endlessly intriguing country."

"Well, it has its drawbacks as a place to live. In Bombay especially, the climate can be trying. It's very humid and generally hot. It's also crowded and noisy. It is quite a shock to the system for many people. But it's certainly never dull."

"How long have you been there?"

"Only a year. This is my first leave. I'm hoping that I'll be there for some considerable time though."

"Are you living on your own?"

"Yes I am. But I'm finding it very different from managing alone in London where I worked for five years before this. I have a large, air-conditioned flat which helps with the climate and I also have efficient servants who take very good care of me. The thought of that upsets some people and when I was telling your father about them, I rather got the impression that he doesn't approve of having others to do your chores for you. Still, employing such people is a fact of Indian life and there are arguments in favour of the system."

"I don't think that you should be too concerned with the opinions of those who have no experience to back them up and are only theorizing. Don't worry about my father. He and my mother are both very sweet but they do tend to take a stern attitude over many issues. I'll try to steer them clear of arguments over supper and we'll hope to keep the conversation light."

Looking down at her small, heart-shaped face, expressive blue eyes and pretty mouth, Bob could not imagine anyone being stern or severe with her.

She did not manage to keep things light. Her parents, with an expert witness to hand, were constitutionally unable to pass over the questions raised by India's history or its current state and both were encouraged by Bob's good sense and local knowledge to explore these in some depth. They were very forceful and Bob, who, at first, kept glancing at her as if regretting her silence and willing her to join in, became immersed in their discussion. Finally, Jess did interrupt her father in mid-sentence.

"Poor Bob! He gave a lecture for you this afternoon. He *is* on leave and probably only for a short time. He must want to forget his work while he is here. How long have you got exactly, Bob?"

"A month. Well! I've had four days already. I'm due back on the first of July. Don't worry about me though. To be truthful, I never do forget India. It has already become a big part of my life but I sometimes feel quite awkward and out of place when I speak about it. I can get carried away and most people aren't that interested. They just look at me and there's a polite silence before they go on to more usual topics. It's been good to open up to your parents. I've enjoyed it."

"Well, now they must let you talk to me for a bit. About other parts of your life! Tell me about yourself. Where are you staying? What about *your* parents? Are they here in Oxford?"

"My mother is. I'm staying at home with her. My father died in 1935. Just after I was born."

"Oh, Bob, I'm so dreadfully sorry. That must have been hard for both of you."

"It was hard for my mother. She was only twenty five, with a young baby. Not for me. I was six months old. I haven't really missed him because I never knew him."

Jess was eager to ask more questions, but Bob, who till now had been so fluent and compelling, became increasingly terse and monosyllabic and was clearly uncomfortable at being the centre of attention and she allowed the conversation to become more general.

By the end of the evening she was sure that she wanted to see more of him and was relieved when he rang the next day to invite her to the theatre. Her parents, having discovered that he was almost thirty years old and knowing that he was capable of thoughtful opinions on important subjects, were pleased that she would have a more mature and worthwhile companion than the rather insubstantial young men she mostly went around with and, if slightly anxious that he might become too serious about her, were reassured by the fact that he would be in England for such a short time. This would be a pleasant interlude before she settled down to the professional life that they wanted for her.

For years afterwards, Jess would recall those last weeks of June, 1964, as a carefree, sunlit succession of picnics in the park, punting on the river and long, lazy lunches in the gardens of picturesque pubs. If there were any showery days, they never clouded her dreamlike images of those outings with Bob. The one shadow that had loomed over her, quickly faded from her mind and did not taint these memories but, for much longer than she later allowed herself to admit, she had been troubled by a rare uncertainty. She always expected things to go her way and had no experience of disappointment but it wasn't easy to gauge Bob's feelings. She found the calm way in which he organised everything wholly satisfying and basked in his unobtrusive management of their time together yet though she grew increasingly sure that these days were more to him than a way of spending his leave agreeably, nothing he did confirmed this. He would give her a swift kiss on her cheek when parting from her but this had a somewhat social and perfunctory air. From the first, he had been committed to prearranged events at home and there were too many days and evenings when he was unable to meet her. She was not invited to any of these family occasions and by the time he was to return to India, had only once, and that accidentally and very briefly, met his mother. Always the centre of both her family and her circle of friends, she found it natural to bring all these elements of her life together and her home was open to everyone. This omission worried her.

Bob was naturally serious and introverted. These traits, which might have been modified by a normal family life, had been strengthened by his special situation. His mother was not unduly possessive or domineering but he recognised from a very early age that he was the focus of her life and happiness and was conscious of the weight of that responsibility. His posting to India was a fortunate diversion. Being at such a distance from home was, in itself, beneficial and his mind was so intensely engaged with his new world that, at last, it escaped its dutiful treadmill and began to learn the habits of freedom. Then, on coming back to England, he was offered a second distraction when he met Jess. She immediately aroused all his well-honed protective instincts simply because she looked so tiny standing beside him but he soon found that her small frame was tightly packed with boundless energy and he was swept along, enchanted, on the irresistible tide of her enthusiasm and gaiety. Sometimes, as he bent to kiss her casually on the cheek and felt her warmth and saw her full, soft lips very close to his, an urge to pull her roughly into his arms and hold on to her seized him, but an innate caution held him back. They hardly knew each other and even contemplating such a possibility and what it could lead to was crazy. He had instantly seen what her parents wanted for her and that did not include flying off to India with him and abandoning all her prospects. Even thinking such thoughts shook him. He must come down to earth and continue on his own chosen pathway, leaving her to discover hers.

She did not go to the airport with him on the day that he left. "It won't be feasible, Jess, because my flight takes off at the crack of dawn. No-one is coming with me. I am saying all my goodbyes beforehand."

"Oh Bob! You will simply vanish without my even seeing you go. It will seem as if this has all been unreal, something that I dreamed. I shall miss you *so* much. It has been such tremendous fun. What will I do when you have gone?"

"You have plenty to do. It won't take you long to find a job that really interests you and you will be amazed at how absorbing you'll find it once you get started."

"I haven't seen any job that could ever be as important to me as yours is to you." There was a slight edge to her voice but she quickly took his hand and looked up at him. "You will write to me won't you?"

"Of course, and I'll look forward to seeing you when I next come home. Meanwhile I'll want to know how things are with you. You must write to me too."

In the many letters he received from her over the next five months, Jess made it clear that she had not settled down as expected. She was temporarily working in a local charity while she continued to look for something permanent but she found something wrong with every post she looked at. Bob was not unaware of the covert message she was sending him. She was telling him something quite other than her obvious news and, while apparently as involved and interested as ever in his own pursuits, he was slowly becoming conscious of a low-grade dissatisfaction eating into him. Every time he heard from Jess this intensified. Although he had a busy official life and was surrounded by crowds of people at formal parties and gatherings, he realised that he was lonely. He began to picture Jess beside him at such affairs or waiting for him when he returned home and he could imagine her bringing his flat to life and lifting it above its current state of soulless workability. He tried not to over-dramatise his feelings, knowing that he was not a man to fall madly in love, but he was drawn to Jess precisely because she had what he lacked – an ability to fling herself instantly and wholeheartedly into everything that she did. He had found her company enlivening and suddenly no-one else seemed especially interesting. Eventually, he was sufficiently discontented to make the first impulsive decision of his life. He applied for special leave, flew home for Christmas, went straight over to see Jess – and asked her to marry him.

Neither the Masons nor his mother were unequivocally pleased when told that he had done this, that she had accepted him and that he wanted to set a date for a wedding as soon as possible, but there were no realistic grounds on which to oppose him and a wedding was planned. He was only home for the Christmas week but would be back again for his annual leave in the summer, so a day was fixed in the third week of June and Jess began to plan the occasion and to get herself ready to fly to India at the beginning of July. Given Bob's age and prospects and her continued failure to find a career, her parents soon decided that this was best for her. His mother had long been steeling herself for the time when he would find someone and though she did not much care for Jess, suspecting that she did not love Bob as she should, could see that she was on the face of it a suitable choice. Mr. and Mrs. Mason managed to be happy about it all and she managed not to be unhappy.

The marriage took place at the massively beautiful Norman church near Jess's home and after a very traditional service, with the heavy scent of flowers wafting around them like incense, the guests, a hundred or so relatives and friends, moved on to a hotel in one of North Oxford's wide, leafy roads for a bridal garden party. Like every event in Jess's life, this went smoothly. It was a perfect day. Later, when she was in Bombay, the Masons would sigh over countless photographs of her in a simple white dress and delicate tiara of white flowers, posing against the dark stonework of the church, holding Bob's arm and smiling up at him or standing in the centre of a sunlit lawn amidst groups of cheerful girls in bright summer dresses.

Jess was eager to start out on her Indian life. "We don't really need a honeymoon, Bob. We are off to faraway places anyway. That will be romantic enough."

"We need a short break first, Jess. I told you from the start that India can be a shock to the system. It may be harder than you realise to settle in there and it won't be a holiday. We'll be plunging straight into our workaday life. Besides, you will have been through all the fuss of the wedding. We will need a few quiet days together in England. Not the seaside. We shall be surrounded by the sea in Bombay. Somewhere in the countryside."

They spent a week in the Lake District. They had known each other for a very short time and for much of that they had been apart. Alone together for the longest period since meeting, they came face to face in a way that had not happened before and those few days set the tone for their whole future together. Bob, once more overcome by a sense of her fragility, was so gentle with Jess that, though she was affectionate and tactile, he did not arouse any passionate response in her. They liked each other, found being together continually interesting and were soon physically at ease with each other. They settled into an agreeable contentment.

On the day that they flew to Bombay, many of their friends turned up unexpectedly at the airport to join their relatives and it was a cheerful and vociferous farewell party. They would be back on leave before too long and Bob had promised Jess that she could always make a trip home if she ever felt excessively homesick. There were no reasons for anyone to be sad.

It was late and already dark when they landed. One of Bob's colleagues whisked them through the manic maelstrom of the Arrivals hall, led them out to a sleek, comfortable car and drove them swiftly into the city.

"I'm not much of a welcoming committee, Jess, but we thought you would be tired and anxious to see your new home. I'll just drop you at the flat. There will be a party in your honour tomorrow evening. You'll meet everyone then. Aziz and Mehdi have prepared a welcome dinner for you, Bob. That's your bearer and cook, Jess, and they have a likely young helper called Gopal. Then, of course, there is your driver, Nicholson. Bob must have already told you about them all. I hope you didn't eat too much on the plane. I think that they've taken a lot of trouble over this meal. They are quite excited, but a bit apprehensive about their new memsahib." He grinned at Jess. "They have been in complete charge of Bob so far and are naturally wondering what his new boss is like."

"Don't tease the poor girl, Mike. Off you go. Ignore him, Jess."

Jess had so far formed only the vaguest impression of Bombay. She came out of the airport into air so steamy and heavy with dust and the scents of spices and smoke that she could almost feel the weight of it, but within seconds they were seated in the car with its own insulated climate and they were only outside in the clammy heat again for the briefest moment before entering the invigorating coolness of the flat. It was like walking onto a film set. Three white-clad servants, waiting in the wide hallway, greeted them with bowed heads and folded palms before moving swiftly to make them comfortable, padding quietly around, putting away luggage and bringing them cold drinks in frosted glasses. Later, sitting in the softly lit dining room where two of the men served the delicious food prepared by their tiny cook, she sighed with pleasure.

"Oh Bob, it's all *so* perfect. I shall love it here."

FOUR

Sam's parents, Zal and Perin Mehta, lived in one of the better parts of Bombay. Even as huge skyscrapers began to stride across the city, filling every open space and reaching into the sky to swallow every vista, their road remained, for a long time, broad and placid, with a fringe of trees that spread welcome patches of shade on the melting tarmac. They finally lost their view of the sea but there were still gardens to look out on and they occasionally heard birds other than the raucous, ubiquitous crows that made every rooftop a noisy, urban forest.

Perin was a simple woman with few outside interests. Keeping her home in order and managing her servants had always been the core of her life, but after her sons, first Sam and then Cyrus, had left to study in England, these domestic duties took on an added importance. When not away at school, the boys had largely been looked after by servants and, when they were young, by reasonably well trained ayahs, but such attention as they had required and their comings and goings had still given her a sense of family life that ended when they were gone. Family in India is never that restricted, however, and, while Zal insisted that a great deal of their time was given to maintaining social links with his business associates, she frequently met her two married sisters and remained very close to her many cousins. She had always been on good, if less affectionate, terms with Zal's relations. Most of them lived in central India but she saw quite a lot of them as they frequently visited Bombay. Zal had come there alone in his early twenties, his ability and ambition outgrowing the opportunities offered by his small home-town and now that he was successful, affluent and a noted figure both within and beyond the Parsi community, the relatives that he had left behind always expected to stay with him when they came to the city and were increasingly turning to him for help in arranging marriages and finding employment for their children. All this meant extra housekeeping chores for Perin and she played a key role in anything to do with engagements and marriages but, though constantly busy, she still missed her sons and eagerly awaited their letters.

One morning, she was in her room, pressing the elaborate sari that she had worn to a party the previous evening. She worked extremely slowly, smoothing every inch of the heavy silk carefully before applying the iron. Slight and rather shabby, in a faded cotton dressing-gown, her short, dark hair unbrushed, she bore no resemblance to the elegant, bejeweled figure that she had presented to fellow guests. That party persona was very much a required element of Zal's self-image and knowing how much this casual appearance and her insistence on performing household tasks irritated him, she felt a spurt of satisfaction. He was a small man but he occupied a large space in her life and in their home and these quiet rebellions fed her sense of her own worth. Her traditional upbringing had imbued her with a belief that open dissent would diminish her but doing jobs that he considered inappropriate allowed her to register a silent protest against his continual demands on her. In any case, she could never bring herself to trust the servants to handle her most precious things; could not trust anyone to be as meticulous as she would always be. She folded the sari in tissue paper and laid it in one of the wide, central drawers of her huge wardrobe, checked again that the emerald necklace that she had worn with it was safely in its luxurious leather box in a smaller drawer and had just locked the cupboard with one of the keys hanging from the heavy chain tied to her belt, when Zal called her into his room.

He had not yet dressed for the office but he was immaculate, having already showered and changed into loose, cotton trousers and a crisp white kurta. His hair was sleek and shining and he exuded a fresh scent of cologne. He never simply sat or indulged in any purposeless activity and, as usual, he was sitting at his large, mahogany desk, already sorting his mail as he sipped his morning tea.

She was a little alarmed by his severe expression. "What is it? Is it bad news?"

He handed her a sheet of paper. "You are always looking for letters from the boys. Well, there you are. Just read that."

Cambridge
5/6/65

Dearest Mummy and Daddy,

I know that you are anxious for my return and are certainly both busily planning ahead for me. You want me to get a suitable job, of course, and I'm fairly sure that you also have ideas about my settling down and finding a wife. I expect that Mummy already has her eye on several good Parsi girls for me. Though I hate to upset and disappoint you, I have to tell you that I want to marry an English girl I have met. Her name is Ann Baker. She isn't a student but is a clever girl. She works in a bookshop here. She was to join her father in his business – he also owns a bookshop – but is prepared to take a chance on me, marry me and come out to India. I know that this will be hard for you and that it will come as a terrible shock because there is so little time before I leave England and I've never told you about Ann before. It is, in fact, the imminence of my return that has finally made us realise how impossible it is for us to part. You will probably believe that we could, and should, forget each other and that, in the end, we could each be content with someone more suitable but we dare not risk losing what seems to us so special. However difficult this is for you and whatever doubts you have, I know that you will both like Ann. She is such a warm, kind-hearted person. Please do understand and help us. I'm very sure about this. I will write again about how we can plan things when I have heard from you.

Your loving son,

Sam.

Perin was very upset by this news but wondered if Zal might not be secretly pleased by it. Many imported goods had been banned in India for some time, becoming a kind of status symbol for anyone able to acquire them and she did not think him above such an attitude to a foreign daughter-in-law. She wasn't immune to a desire to impress people with her sons' wives and she had, indeed, already seen daughters of notable Parsi families who would be ideal. Naturally a girl should be good looking. Sam had said nothing about Ann's looks. She would obviously be fair-skinned and that was something. He said that she was clever. That sounded faintly alarming, though, of course, girls too should be well educated. Perin was not thinking consciously of all that she had endured at the hands of a husband more intellectual and quicker witted than herself but it had been a wounding experience and cleverness did not seem to her to be all that good for the character. Sam did say, though, that Ann was kind. She had always believed that it was possible to get along with a large-hearted person.

Whatever Zal's deeper reactions to their son's letter might be, for the moment he was definitely ruffled. "This is really too bad of Sam. I trusted both boys to be sensible in these matters. I had long talks with them before they left and set out all such possibilities. I warned them against any rash behaviour. I shall have to meet this girl and her family and see what is to be done."

"You are very right. Sam hasn't said much about Ann's family. He is caught up with this matter of love but there is much more to think about. Whatever this girl is like, it is important to know what her background is, what sort of people these are."

"Certainly it is. I must go to England immediately. I shall leave as soon as it can be arranged."

"Zal! We have my sister's big party next week. She is counting on us."

"It won't be possible to go. This affair of Sam is of the first importance. You must call and tell her that I will be abroad."

"I'll call after breakfast. Poor dear, she will be quite cut-up but she will understand when I tell her about Sam."

"Don't say anything, Perin, until I have gone further into the matter. Say that I have to go to England on business. Don't discuss this with anyone."

"No. No. You are very right. Better to say nothing as yet. We will tell everyone only when things are quite decided. Maybe Sam will think better of it. God is great."

When bent on a course of action, Zal was unstoppable. Arrangements for his flight and accommodation in England were made with the efficiency and speed that his many connections made possible and he left a week after this conversation. Perin, alone with her troubled thoughts and obedient to his prohibition, was unable to find any relief by talking things over with her relatives as she would normally have done. She might in theory trust in God's power to change Sam's mind but fears about his future and questions about this girl whom he said he loved weighed heavily on hers. What sort of people would he find himself involved with? Where and how did they live?

Ann's maternal grandfather, Arthur Fincham, was, in fact, a prosperous farmer and when his daughter, Edna, had married Clifford Baker, the son of a neighbouring farmer, he had given her a large cottage, set in an acre of land, and this was still her home. Edna Baker's life was not, in its essentials, dissimilar to that of Perin Mehta. She, too, though sensible and shrewd, was a simple woman whose energies were largely expended on her house and family. Her husband also was more intellectual and wide-ranging in his interests than she was but, where Zal had found it necessary to move away from his small town, Clifford had found room for personal expansion within his rural environment and, because they were still anchored within the circle that had held them close from birth, the Bakers' marriage was friendlier and more contented than that of the Mehtas. Their minds moved at different speeds but their blood beat to the slow, shared rhythm of their country heritage.

That heritage had never guaranteed immunity from problems. They knew of family break-ups and difficult adolescents but such things were rarer and somehow less disastrous in their small world and they were both totally unprepared for the blow that they now endured.

Edna, unlike Clifford, had never taken Ann's placidity for granted. She had memories of her docile toddler caught up in sudden, private fascinations that left her deaf to anything that her mother might say, but she had expected any similar, adult aberration to be mild and temporary. She had certainly believed Clifford fully capable of dealing with anything untoward in their lives yet during the dreadful day when Ann revealed her unsuspected friendship with Sam and her determination not only to marry him but to go with him to India, she saw her husband devastated by these disclosures. Indeed, they were all so worn out by this unlooked for breakdown in their smooth dealings with each other that they could hardly bear to be together and after she had broken her news, Ann did not stay on as planned but, in an uncharacteristically dramatic gesture, went straight back to Cambridge. When they were alone again, Clifford and Edna sat and held hands. No warnings, no pleas for caution, no appeal for a period of reflection on the risks she was facing had penetrated Ann's certainty.

"She's gone. I don't mean back to Cambridge. She's gone forever. We've already lost her." Clifford's tone was bleak. "She's been through all this without our knowing a thing about it. She's cut us out of her life. Even if we could persuade her to reconsider, she'd never feel the same about us again. She's left us. She doesn't have to travel to India to do that."

Unusually within his family, farmers for generations, Clifford had been a studious boy and a voracious reader. This had not caused him any problem because he was also strong and sturdy and adept at sport, a useful member of the football team and something of a star player at the local tennis club. However, in his early twenties it became apparent that he had no heart for working on their large farm, which would eventually be managed by his elder brother, James. His father had found what seemed an equitable and suitable solution by setting him up in the nearby town's one small bookshop when it came up for sale. It had its limitations but Clifford had made a success of it and, through the purchase and sale of rare and specialist books, had become involved in a wider world. His shop was the public face of a hidden, internal life that had been nourished by the dream of passing everything to his daughter. He kept this passionate, inner self contained within the conventional facade of a small town businessman, but the prospect of opening up to Ann in a shared working future had helped to sustain it. Her defection ended these hopes and, for a while, it seemed like the destruction of all he felt himself to be.

Edna's feelings were more straightforward. She experienced a pang whenever she thought of Ann at such a great distance from them but, overwhelmingly, she was stricken by the idea of their apparently successful family unit on display as a failure. For the first time in her life she envisaged her relations and friends as critical and hostile and longed to escape, to be elsewhere. The frightening thing was, that for her there had never been anywhere else and this unfamiliar and uncomfortable sense of narrow horizons was heightened by a further trial, for almost immediately after her brief disruptive visit, another note arrived from Ann.

14/6/65

Just to tell you that Sam's father, Zal, is coming to England. He will be staying here at the Royal Cambridge overnight. He is clearly coming to inspect me and hopes to meet you. Since you obviously will not want him to come to you and as it is easy for you to get to Cambridge, it seems a good idea for us to meet for lunch at his hotel. That will be on the 20th. Let me know if you will be coming. I know that you hate all this, but it is something that has to be done and you will only need to stay a short time.

Ann.

"Everything is so rushed." Edna's voice trembled. She found it hard to believe that this letter, with its cold, unfriendly tone, could have anything to do with her daughter. "Here was Ann, only two days ago, telling us that she wants to marry some unknown foreigner and going off without saying anything about our meeting *him,* only to turn round and ask us to meet his father. And he's coming all this way without knowing if we will or not. And I don't want to."

It was years since Clifford had heard this plaintive, girlish tone from his wife. "You can't blame him for coming. He must be as anxious about Sam as we are about Ann. I certainly want to see what sort of man he is and find out a lot more about the whole family. I want to know exactly what Ann is getting herself into. I've never heard of his religion but since he's sent his son to Cambridge, he must be modern and well-to-do. And we will have a good chance to see what Sam is like. It won't change things. I feel sure there is nothing any of us can do. I've told you that we've already lost her whatever happens. We'll never go back to how things were. All we can do is try to see her through this and make sure that things are done as sensibly as possible. Then, whatever we feel, we'll just have to stand by her if things don't work out."

He put a consoling arm round her shoulder. "There's no help for it. You'll manage alright, dear. You've never let me down yet. We have to go."

As they went into the hotel on the appointed morning, Edna's heart lurched at the sight of the two exotic males awaiting them. They clearly belonged somewhere it was impossible for her to picture. Ann's obvious ease with them suddenly made her betrayal tangible. Edna looked at Clifford. For so long he had been the significant masculine presence in his daughter's life and, though they had shared interests from which she herself had been excluded, she had never resented their closeness and was shattered by the realisation that this, for him, was bereavement. She went through the introductions, the finding of a table and the choosing of food in a blur. It was an ordeal and at the end of their meal she realised that it was not yet over.

"Sam, Ann's parents and I need to speak privately." Zal's voice was firm. "I think we all know that you will not be persuaded to change your minds but we need to discuss the matter without you. Why don't you both go into town and come back in an hour or so. We'll have our coffee in the lounge and talk things over."

Clifford nodded his agreement. Both men were led by habits of command and authority to attempt to take charge. Clifford, broad-shouldered and bulky, had a strong presence but Zal, small and dapper, was no less forceful. Ann and Sam went off obediently and Edna sat down quietly at the coffee table.

"Let me make something clear." Zal looked directly at Clifford. "Apart from your other worries, you must wonder what Sam can be offering Ann. He is only just completing his education and his future is unsettled. All this emotional turmoil has blinded him to such realities. But there is nothing to fear in that regard. I have a wide range of valuable contacts and whatever happens, he will find a worthwhile post. You can be assured of Ann's material welfare. Then, too, we shall help Sam when it comes to finding them a home."

"Well, all that is important to us, naturally," Clifford was equally direct, "but it's not our first priority. Ann has had a comfortable life and she had a good future prepared for her that she is simply throwing away, but it's this leap into the unknown, the loss of all that she is used to that we're troubled about."

"It might be an idea for her to come out to us for a visit before we think of any wedding." Zal glanced at Edna. "There are real difficulties involved in setting up anything in the short time we have and that way she would have a chance to see what India is like and get to know our family before she commits herself."

"No! I can't agree to that." Clifford sounded quite belligerent. "She has made up her mind and I'm sure that she has the character to deal with whatever that leads her into. I need to see her married before she goes off on this venture. We have to know where we stand once and for all."

Zal, discerning an irrational, underlying bitterness that led Clifford to reject any possibility of reclaiming his daughter, felt unable to argue. "So! Would you want her to be married from home? There is the problem of religious difference. I understand that Ann has told you something about us Parsis and our customs. We are not a strictly religious family and she need not be nervous on that account. We shall not make the kind of demands on her that occur in some families but we do keep to our community ways. Possibly a civil ceremony would meet that difficulty."

"If this does go ahead, that's definitely what we would prefer and, in the circumstances, I think that only we and any of Sam's family you invite should be there and that it should take place in Cambridge." Clifford turned to Edna. "Wouldn't that be the best thing?"

She stared at her hands which were clenched tightly in her lap. It would be the worst thing. What was happening to them? All their old certainties seemed swallowed up by a sick sensitivity to other people's attitudes that left them cut off from any normal feelings about Ann and made her wedding an embarrassment. They dreaded inviting their family and friends to it but later they might regret this lack of courage. She looked up. Clifford's face was tense and there was a glint of shame in his eyes. She was pierced with sadness. It was not in him to parade his feelings of hurt and rejection but he was clearly capable of retaliation. This decision was a final word to Ann. It was hateful to think of him behaving in such a way but she simply could not add to his distress. She nodded slowly. "Yes it's the best thing to do."

Perin had spent an anxious and lonely time back in Bombay, unrelieved by any comforting get-togethers with her sisters, but though relieved when she got a letter from Zal, her hands were trembling as she opened it.

London
21/6/65

Dear Perin,

I had a comfortable flight and arrived on time. Cyrus met me at the airport and as soon as we reached my hotel, we telephoned Sam to confirm that I would be with him in Cambridge the following day. I met Ann in the afternoon and have to tell you that she is a very attractive and pleasant girl and there is nothing to worry about as far as she personally is concerned. I spent the evening alone with Sam. He is sorry to cause us so much anxiety but in his quiet way very determined. It is clear, as he himself realises, that his impending return has forced the issue. He only met Ann around eight months ago. If they had met sooner and known each other longer who can say what might have happened. They may have thought more carefully about what they were undertaking. As it is, their emotions are heightened within what is something of a hothouse atmosphere. It will, though, be best to accept a girl who, apart from being a non-Parsi, seems in every way suitable and agreeable, than to take the slightest risk of losing our son. How must it be for

Mr. and Mrs. Baker who face losing their daughter? They are very decent people. Mr. Baker, though not perhaps exactly wealthy, seems very well placed. I can tell that they have been used to an uneventful family life and that Ann has always been a loving and dutiful daughter. They put on a brave face but I believe them to be in a state of shock, sleepwalking their way through this situation. It seems accepted that Sam will bring Ann home with him and her father is adamant that she must be married before she comes. Given that Sam has put us in such an impossible position by making his plans known so late in the day and that we have very little time to fix everything, we eventually decided that a quiet registry wedding, immediately before they leave England, is the most viable solution to all our problems. I know that you will be very grieved about this but we can have our own celebration in India later. In this way Ann's parents will not have to go through an elaborate ceremony for which they plainly have no heart. Indeed they don't even want this simple affair to take place in their own town but in Cambridge. I wouldn't go so far as to say that they are ashamed of what their daughter is doing but they obviously worry about what their family and friends will think. The plan for a civil wedding will be the least upsetting for them. We will certainly arrange something more significant to give the young ones a good start in Bombay. I had assumed they would fly out but they will apparently have considerable baggage and want to come by sea. You will not believe it but Sam, who has never ventured near a kitchen in his life, has been on a shopping spree,

*buying an unbelievable quantity of household goods.
Does he think he can tie Ann down with a weight of
domestic apparatus? What has happened to our son?
He may have been somewhat wilful occasionally but
never less than sensible. This is a hasty letter but I am
giving you as full a picture as possible. We will go into
details when I get back. Cyrus is well. It is a great joy to
be spending unexpected time with him in London. He
is a dear boy and doing brilliantly at his studies. We
must just hope that Sam's future will not be harmed by
all this. We shall have to do what we can to see that he
progresses in the best possible way. I will now be with
you on the 26th. My flight arrives at nine a.m. I hope it
arrives on time. Please send the car to be at the airport
by eight thirty.*

Zal.

Sam's unconventional wedding was no longer something
that might not happen. He would not change his mind. Perin
had always dreamed of a long, pleasurable period in which
she and any future daughter-in-law would slowly get to
know each other, enclosed in the familiar, female world that
they had both inherited, until all their joint planning ended
in the appropriate and traditional rituals. Now, her son was
about to bring home a stranger who, with scant formality,
would have already become his wife. Disappointment was
a dull ache deep inside her and, fretted by thoughts of her
obligation to accommodate unknown ways and provide
unusual comforts, she was thrown into a frenzy of house
cleaning and reorganistion. She could not relax and her
servants were constantly harried. Zal returned to a less than

peaceful home and found himself displaced as the centre of their domestic arrangements. He could only find refuge in his own room which did remain exempt from all this activity, hoping that, once Sam arrived and Perin had met Ann, calm would be restored.

FIVE

"Do you know what my father has done now?" Ann, brandishing a letter, was red-faced and angry. "Without asking me what I want to do, he's sorting and packing my books and has got my mother to pick the things they believe I shall want to take with me. They can't wait to get rid of me."

Faced with separation from Sam, her decision to go to India had been a simple, compelling necessity but there was too much time between making that decision and being able to carry it out. Moving to a new country and planning a marriage involved bureaucratic procedures that lowered the emotional temperature and brought her up against practicalities. The strain of all this was throwing her off balance. Her feelings towards her parents had hardened, causing her to dwell on every perceived slight. She did not look forward to going home and decided to continue working till the last possible moment before her wedding, making her final stay there a short one. She informed her mother and father of her plan somewhat defiantly, hoping, even believing, that they would attempt to overrule her and was unreasonably hurt when they did nothing to persuade her to change her mind. She was increasingly nervy and touchy.

"Calm down." Sam took her hand. "You are being really unfair. After you told them that you intended to go back for such a short time and so soon before we leave, they obviously had to begin your packing. You should have arranged to go home much earlier if you wanted to deal with it."

"They can deal with it. My father has always managed everything. He can cope without me. I shan't go home at all. You know that they don't really want me there."

"How can I know what they want? I don't know them at all." Sam was horrified by this intransigence. "I do know that this isn't right. I feel that we should both visit them and that I should meet all your relatives but I've accepted that you won't allow that. I don't want to push you over your reasons. I'm trying to understand and don't want to make things harder for you than they need to be. I try to remember that we'll have years ahead of us to put everything right and get people to accept what we are doing. But you have to go home. This really isn't the way to behave."

"I'm not going, Sam. I can't be with them, feeling as I do, as they do. Too much has changed. It would all be a miserable pretence. You know full well that they hate what we are doing. They don't even want anyone to come to my wedding. They want it to be a hole-in-the-corner affair."

"Ann, they've accepted a marriage. It doesn't matter what form it takes. That's not the important part of what we want. It was never going to be the conventional, joyous occasion. They have to get through it in any way that they can."

"Well, they are ignoring my deepest feelings. I won't trouble myself over theirs."

"But I am troubled over them. And what about your grandparents? It is your duty to see them at such a time in your life."

"Don't talk to me about duty, Sam. That sounds very Indian to me."

Sam looked as if she had struck him. She had never made a critical reference to his nationality, his beliefs or any implicit difference between them before. She ignored his dismay.

"What about their duty to me?" she sounded furious. "They are keeping very quiet. I don't know how they feel about us. They aren't making any push to see us married. They are asking no questions. They are simply opting for an easy life."

Her grandparents, on both sides, had always been there, a continuous and reassuring background presence and, though, in their stolid way, they had never done more than accept her into their daily routines, she had taken their affection for granted. Torn between wanting to see them and fearing how they would behave towards her, she felt that they too were letting her down just when she needed them most.

Sam was deeply shocked and alarmed to think that they would begin their life together even more discordantly than he had anticipated. What had happened to the warm, gentle Ann that he loved? The change in her parents must be deeper and more wounding than he had realised. He was seriously disturbed by his part in all this but consoled himself with the thought that, once they were settled, they could invite his in-laws to India and come back to stay with them in England and mend all these broken ties. They had expected problems. They would work things out.

Amidst all this friction his graduation was a welcome break, shared with his brother, who came for the day to support him. It felt good to introduce Ann to someone in his family who was unaffected by all this dissension and she was glad of company. Cyrus was a courteous and personable escort. He was shorter and broader than Sam, with very fair skin and a hint of plumpness that rounded and somewhat blurred his features. He reminded Ann of his father but he was smoother, less direct in manner than either Zal or Sam. Whenever she spoke he leaned in towards her as if totally focused on her every word, but she noticed that his replies betrayed a degree of inattentiveness. She could picture him as the doctor he would become; soothing his patients with a flattering bedside manner while his mind was off on its own track, making its decisions for them.

Zal had instructed his sons to ensure that there was a suitable record of this event for the family album and after the ceremony was over and they emerged from the hall there was a flurry of photography before they walked to the centre of town. Cyrus was catching a late train back to London and they wanted a leisurely meal together before he left. The restaurant was full of students and their families and conversation in such surroundings was something of a struggle but Ann felt that this wasn't the only reason for Sam's retreat into his earlier guardedness. These brothers were not exactly open with each other. Were all the Mehtas like this? How would she ever really know them? She felt the prick of tears. She had only just discovered that she didn't even know her own family.

"Ann." Sam brought her back into the conversation. "I'm just telling Cyrus about the wedding arrangements."

"It will be a very simple affair." Ann hated the apologetic note in her voice. "There'll just be you, my parents and two of Sam's friends as witnesses. I'm sure that it won't be anything like an Indian wedding."

"You are lucky to escape the full Parsi parade," Cyrus risked a humorous tone, "with our mother and her sisters as commanding officers. Though you deserve a parade, Ann. I'm speaking as a younger brother and a loyal but clear-sighted citizen. You are already taking on Sam and it's quite something to take on India too. It isn't a country for the faint-hearted. Then, on top of all that, you will have to deal with the Parsi community which, admirable as it is and great as its achievements are, has its little ways." He caught Sam's fierce glare and stopped short. Sam was always so intense. At home, although always dutiful and obedient, his brother had somehow radiated an air of latent mutiny that generated constant underlying tension between him and their father. This had worked greatly to his own advantage for their concentration on each other had meant an easier time for him as the younger son. Slipping under the radar, lavish with endearments and smiles, he had always managed to do much as he pleased. In London, he went about with plenty of girls who offered agreeable company but nothing was known about them at home and he would never dream of taking them seriously. In fact, he deliberately chose girls who did not take themselves seriously and posed no danger of any complications. *His* future wife would smooth his path not cause him difficulties. Why couldn't Sam do as he did? The confrontation with their parents over Ann had not been necessary. He looked at her. What was it about her that had drawn Sam into this? Though taller than he found feminine and somewhat sturdily built, she moved gracefully, with a natural, unselfconscious elegance. Her straight, shoulder length hair was thick and glossy and her complexion clear and fresh. She was undeniably attractive but there was nothing especially striking about her apart from her eyes, which were an unusual green. At first sight she had struck him as somewhat shy and diffident but he quickly noted that she had a direct, almost appraising, way of looking at people and that there was a very firm set to her chin. There was probably a determination and strength in her which appealed to Sam who, on the point of losing the unaccustomed freedom that he had enjoyed in Cambridge all this time, faced trying to forge an independent life for himself in the teeth of the restraints he had always known at home. The idea of a staunch ally must be very enticing. Cyrus rarely allowed himself strong emotions but he was somehow moved by the thought of what awaited Ann and turned impulsively towards her. "You are a brave girl. I'll be proud to see you married."

It was, in the end, a rather sad little wedding and his presence on the day did much to help ease them through it. Sam would have seemed alien and lonely without him there and he provided a buffer between Ann and her parents and a welcome, neutral, companion for the two witnesses. The Registry Office had a chilly, uninviting air and such a small party was rather lost among the many utilitarian chairs set out within its unadorned space. After a brief glance at Sam, who was also stiff and serious, Ann stood tense and unsmiling throughout and did not look at anyone other than the registrar, whose words sounded to her more like the official rubber stamping of her great decision than any kind of endorsement or blessing. This was another necessary task summarily completed. She was relieved when it was over.

Their ship sailed from Liverpool the following day, and her parents drove them to the docks and came on board with them as they found their cabin and stowed their hand luggage. This brief reunion with their daughter and impossibly slight contact with Sam should have been unbearable for the Bakers but their habits of reticence and restraint enabled them to carry it off with considerable dignity. They had gone through the registry rites with good grace, been heroically sociable at a simple, post-wedding lunch and endured an overnight stay in the newlyweds' hotel. They were intensely unhappy and apprehensive about Ann's future but, guiltily conscious that their inability to allow her to marry on home ground had been a failure of nerve that had resulted in this unsatisfying, cursory affair, were trying to make some amends by seeing her off bravely. Clifford's pronouncement on Ann – "She's gone. She's left us." – seemed to have been proved by these last difficult weeks, but Cambridge had been so near. She had still been within reach physically. Only when all visitors on board were asked to go ashore, did the full reality of separation finally catch her parents' hearts and stop their breath. But habit again prevailed. The boom of the foghorn sounded doom-laden and melancholy but there were no tears and no overt drama. Clifford shook Sam's hand and held Ann close for several moments. Edna hugged Ann and gave Sam a quick kiss on the cheek.

They walked away from the ship without a single glance back to where Ann stood tensely at the rail and drove away from the docks without a word but, suddenly, a few miles into their journey, Clifford pulled into a lay-by and stopped. Edna, looking at him in surprise, was horrified to see that he was silently weeping.

"Don't, Clifford! Oh my dear, please don't. You will see her again. Sam seems a decent young man. She'll be alright. He'll look after her."

"I hope so." Clifford wiped his face. It was bad enough that Edna had seen him in tears. It was impossible to admit that, whatever common sense told him, he had seen himself as the one to look after his daughter and at some primitive level had felt that he would always do so. "As I said before, if things go wrong of course we will stand by her and help her." He took a deep breath. "Now though, I can't bear to think about her. All these years of talking things over together and I have nothing to say to her. Nothing I want to hear her say."

SIX

The ship docked in Bombay in the early hours of the morning. Outside their cabin door there was a great deal of commotion. A rather flustered steward arrived with a tray of tea and toast and Sam, who was already dressed, ate and drank as usual but Ann's stomach lurched and she felt slightly sick at the thought of food. The voyage had lasted three weeks – three weeks of blissful freedom. During the long, bright days she had floated through a round of social events in a contented haze, knowing that this was probably the only time they would ever have completely to themselves; a time on neutral ground, away from all those who had influence over them or ties with which to pull at them. But she had not forgotten what such pressures could do to them and, now, after her taste of carefree happiness, the thought of facing them again, in a strange place and an unfamiliar guise, was more daunting than she had expected.

"You must at least drink some tea." Sam handed her a cup. "You are in for something of an ordeal. I won't try to describe what officialdom has in store for us but I have been on deck and seen our welcome party waiting to come on board. That will be hectic enough."

In contrast to their low key departure, their arrival was, indeed, something of a carnival. Ann had no idea who all the people were who rushed upon them, hugging and kissing her and festooning her with the heady garlands they carried. She instinctively drew back from such instant intimacy but she wanted to make a good impression and forced herself to accept these gestures. Zal's face was reassuringly familiar and it was a relief to find that Sam's mother was blessedly restrained and less voluble than the others and, once the excitement had died down, she took everyone away with her, leaving Sam, Zal and Ann to go through the lengthy procedures of arrival. Fortunately, Zal knew an official who speeded up the process but it was only after two exhausting, sweaty hours that they finally came out of the customs shed. Perin had arranged to send the car back for them and the driver, waving to attract their attention, led them over to it.

Worn out by the noise and continual movement they had emerged from, Ann felt a huge relief as she sank into her seat but it was a brief respite, for on leaving the docks, they plunged into the roaring mayhem of chaotic traffic. Left and right sides of the road blurred in a confused melee of wildly hooting vehicles with unbelievably serene pedestrians threading between them. Wherever a space opened up, there was a crazed convergence on it from all sides. Zal, sitting in front next to the driver, was unmoved but Ann, in the rear with Sam, cringed from the window and edged closer to him. The quiet shade of the road that they finally reached seemed unreal, impossible.

Zal pointed to a square, grey building ahead. "There we are. That's Dahanipur House. We're home."

They drove past the imposing facade and solid front door and drew up at a side entrance. The driver took the car off to the basement garage and they went up a shallow stone stairway into a dark hall, got into an antique lift and clanked up to the second floor where they were met by another flurry of greetings and garlands and borne into a large, opulent room on a wave of excitement. Zal allowed this to continue for a few minutes and then took them all in hand. Explaining that the heavy baggage, carried in a hired truck, had arrived and that he and Sam were going downstairs to organise its disposal before lunch could be served, he clapped his hands and three white-clad servants came forward with trays of snacks and drinks. They moved round the room with carefully expressionless faces and lowered eyes but they could not resist surreptitious glances at Ann. Perin spoke sharply to them, then, having made sure that everyone was comfortable, also excused herself and took Ann through to a large en-suite bedroom at the back of the flat where for the first time they were alone.

"This is your room, Ann. It will take time to find your own place and I hope that you will be comfortable while you are with us. I've put a desk for Sam and these two chairs. You are probably accustomed to being on your own a lot. We usually sit together in the balcony in the evenings but if you need to be private, Sam can always join you here."

"It's lovely." There was an awkward pause. "I'm not sure what I should call you." Ann looked warily at her mother-in-law. "Would you find it odd if I called you Perin? I don't want to be unfeeling or rude but you know nothing about me and it's going to take time for us to mean anything to each other. We share one thing. We both love Sam. I know what a disappointment I am to you but I want you to be sure of that. I do love Sam."

"Yes, of course. It's all so different now. When I was married, love wasn't the important thing. We Parsis have generally been freer than other Indian women but family background was always a big consideration in these affairs. I can't say that all our marriages worked out well but we rarely considered letting that be known and we always had something solid to fall back on whenever we were unhappy; a social standing and family connections to hold on to whatever happened. I expect that seems strange to you, difficult to understand."

"No. It isn't difficult. But there isn't really any perfect way to choose someone for life is there? People will make mistakes however they do it. I believe that this is right for Sam and me but I can only promise to do my best." Ann hesitated, "Can I confess something to you? Things were very tense at home recently. Now I've had time to think more calmly about what I've done to my parents, I feel bad about it and that's why I would find it hard to call anyone else Mother or Father."

Perin made a move towards her but stopped abruptly. "Well maybe you'll soon have some good news for us."

"Good news?" Ann was puzzled.

"I hope that it won't be too long before I'm a grandmother. That will solve the problem of what to call me."

Sam came into the room at that moment, a strained look on his face. "It's a bit early to be talking about good news already. Let the poor girl settle in. She's got plenty to deal with."

"Well, I've got lunch to deal with. I can't leave the servants to themselves on such an important day. I hope you won't find our food too spicy, Ann. I've tried to have a few bland dishes. We'll eat in about fifteen minutes. Just freshen up and you can sort out your things and have a rest this afternoon." Perin went out without looking at Sam.

He took Ann in his arms. "Are you alright? I hope that my mother hasn't said anything to upset you. She's more emotional right now than she seems. You'll have to treat her gently for a while."

Ann stroked his face. "Relax, Sam. You needn't feel that you have to watch us all the time. We'll get used to each other. We'll be fine. It's probably a good idea to start by being on time for lunch. I'll just wash and tidy up."

The dining room was very grand. A long, highly polished table stood in the centre of a wide expanse of black and white tiled flooring. Three stiff floral arrangements were carefully set along its centre under three pendant light fittings. On two ornately carved, semi-circular tables on the side walls, there were equally formidable arrangements, flanked by silver bowls piled high with fruit.

The behaviour of the guests was far less formal than the setting. There was an uninhibited bustle as they came into the room. Zal, already at the head of the table, was calling loudly for Sam and Ann to come and take the chairs on either side of him and everyone else was instructing others where to sit, ignoring Perin's attempts to set them right, but eventually the voluble commotion subsided and they all found a seat. Two uniformed but bare-footed servants padded round with large serving dishes. Everyone called out to Ann with advice on what she should eat – Zal even putting some food onto her plate.

"Let her take her time and decide for herself what she wants." Sam sounded anxious. " She isn't used to all this fuss."

They turned their attention to him and Ann was free to look around and begin to gather who all the members of this exuberant welcoming committee were, though their unfamiliar names mostly eluded her. She managed to identify Perin's two sisters and their husbands and a cousin who clearly shared boyhood memories with Sam. A short restless man called Behram seemed to be Zal's nephew and was apparently on a visit to Bombay and staying in the flat. To her right, was a slender, striking woman who had said very little and taken no part in the general hubbub.

"I'm afraid we're rather an excitable lot." This neighbour turned to her with a rueful smile. "You must find us overwhelming. I'm Perin's cousin, Freni. I've been staying with her for a few days. I'd have liked to get to know you but unfortunately I'm going back home to Delhi tonight. I'm sure though, that we'll meet again sometime. I don't get to Bombay very often but maybe one day you will be able to visit me and…."

Behram interrupted her. He had been taking photographs of them all at the table. "I think I've got some good shots here of us at the docks and of your arrival at the flat, Ann. I'll let you have copies and you can send them to your people."

"Thank you."

Ann did not intend to thrust these pictures on her parents. She could, at last, acknowledge that there were forgivable reasons for their concern. India, to her relatives, was not a place that could realistically be home. Though not ignorant, they were unimaginative and would find it hard to picture the daily lives of people so foreign to them. Her mother and father were struggling to overcome serious reservations about the Mehtas and she had added to their difficulties by refusing to allow them to get to know Sam. Their doubts had roused such a fierce aggression in her that she had made no concessions. She had totally withdrawn from them. She had not behaved well. She had to treat them more gently. Photographs would graphically confront them with the strangeness of her new life; her distance from them. For a while she would only send carefully worded descriptions of what was happening here.

As the weeks passed, this increasingly seemed to her a sensible decision. She admitted to herself that life with the in-laws was a cliché but the heat, noise and alien cultural norms she was coping with made it less shop worn. She was told that this was a cool season in Bombay but continuing high temperatures exacerbated by humidity sapped her energy and the constant background noise, like a sort of oriental tinnitus, was hard to get used to. There never seemed any possibility of being quiet and alone. No one ever closed doors. Zal and Perin, and the relatives who frequently stayed with them, always slept with their bedrooms open to the passageways. When Sam closed their door, Ann was stricken with self-consciousness. Unable to shake off her sense of shadowy watchers around them, she conjured up an atmosphere of sly prurience and could no longer respond naturally to Sam, who was sometimes sharp with her. She dreaded giving any sign of a quarrel.

"Shush, Sam."

"Don't be silly. No one's listening to us. They're all asleep. Come here."

Sam, so dismissive of others at night, was all too aware of them by day. His anxiety over any actual or potential misunderstanding between his family and Ann made him alert to, and critical of, any small slip on either side. This caused irritation all round and often left Ann feeling bruised and shaken. Their romantic visions were being severely tested and her resentment could not always be concealed.

"You don't love me, Sam."

"You know that's not true. You're everything to me."

"Yes! Yes! Love is what all this is supposed to be about. You certainly have strong feelings for me – but love? You love the effect that I have on you. You love the idea of my loving you. You love the image of yourself breaking free and braving your family for me – though I don't know that you have done that exactly – but you couldn't be so harsh if you really loved me."

In spite of her rare outbursts of frustration, they always managed to neutralize and put aside these disagreements, oblivious to any darkness they were storing inside. They had many good times. Going off for the day together to explore the city, they would recapture all the harmony of their Cambridge days and, sent on two occasions for weekends alone in a seaside chalet owned by Zal's company, they re-entered the secret, passionate space in which simply resting against each other could banish every dissatisfaction and heal any pain.

Throughout October, Sam was frequently in meetings connected with his job-search and Ann spent a lot of time with her mother-in-law. A belated wedding reception, planned as a celebration with all the Mehtas' relatives and friends, was of first importance to Perin and had been booked for the twenty fifth of November at the city's main hotel, the Taj Mahal. Ann could not be persuaded to wear a sari for the occasion – any photographs taken at this party would have to be sent home and she felt that this would be too much for her parents – but she admitted that her simple wardrobe contained nothing suitable, so she and Perin set out on a round of shopping. She had always worn good quality but somewhat dowdy clothes and buying them had been a pedestrian activity. Now, she found herself in an entirely new world where what would have been considered frivolous at home was taken very seriously. There was nothing haphazard about their outings. Each was as meticulously planned as a polar expedition. Perin had a long list of essential fabric stores. In shop after shop, bales of gorgeous cloth were unrolled and rivers of silk and satin flowed over counters in front of them. Ann soon decided on a length of turquoise raw silk but it could only finally be purchased after they had seen everything on offer. Nothing could be decided until every possibility had been examined and every price compared and bargained over.

Once the material was bought, it had to be made up into an evening dress by Perin's tailor, who came regularly to the flat for fittings. These took place in the verandah, with all the family asked for their opinion and servants usually somewhere on the sidelines. Then, the tailoring in hand, Perin took Ann off to search for shoes and accessories to complement this important dress. Any strain between them was forgotten and they enjoyed themselves hugely.

In the first week of November, Sam accepted a senior post in the Finance Department of a company that made rubber components for the motor industry and was to start work on the first of December. They had, by then, already spent considerable time flat hunting and Ann, who was trying not to be too plainly horrified by the din and squalor of

Bombay, was relieved when they managed to find something acceptable on the top floor of a four storey building on the shoreline. Though this was on a very busy road lined with small shops, the flat itself was at the rear of the block, overlooking the sea, and so comparatively peaceful. The building, grey, salt-stained and far from imposing, was called "Sea King." Ann, delighted by the determined poetry of many Indian names and expressions in the face of a very prosaic reality, was certainly amused by, and irrationally influenced by it. A more practical consideration was that, like Dahanipur House, this was an older building with spacious rooms and several storerooms behind the kitchen which Ann, having seen the cramped and dingy servants' quarters in the basement, meant to convert into more salubrious accommodation for anyone she might eventually employ.

Perin's father, who had died when his grandsons were teenagers, had left money in trust to be given to them when they married and this sum, supplemented by Zal's promised help, enabled Sam to complete the purchase quickly. Clifford's pride had overridden his hurt feelings and he had given Ann a substantial amount as a wedding present. He had intended this to be used towards her new home but when he understood the byzantine bureaucracy involved in the foreign ownership of property (and he had to deal with the idea of Ann as a foreigner), he had insisted that she put it into a personal account that would give her some independence and free her from the influence of her in-laws. Zal was, indeed, already making suggestions about decor but Perin was unusually firm with him on this point.

"We will lend them the bare essentials, a bed, a table, some chairs. Then Ann can take her time to arrange things to suit herself. Don't forget that she is used to being active, to working full time. She will need something substantial to do while Sam is settling into his work. This way too, she will learn to do things here on her own. That will be good for her. Good for both of them."

They were married. Sam had a job. They were property owners. The function on the twenty fifth became a triple celebration. It was a suitably grand affair. There was a bad moment when, looking around the bright assembly of elegant strangers, Ann recalled the spartan Registry Office, its plain furniture, the small sober group in attendance and her heart contracted, but she was immediately drawn back into the gaiety and goodwill around her. She herself was transformed. Her brown hair had been newly cut in a short, sharp style that emphasised her one real beauty, her large green eyes, and, glamorous in her new finery, she was the confident centre of attention and determinedly cast off any sadness.

After this tremendous party, all the excitement died down. Though Christmas was an important part of the local calendar and all the hotels provided elaborate buffets, Ann felt that to acknowledge it would be too painful. So they ignored it. December was a quiet month. Sam bought a secondhand car and drove to work daily. Ann was getting ready to move. All their heavy baggage still lay unopened in a back storeroom and could be easily transported. On the second of January, three months after their arrival, they spent their first night in the new flat.

Curled up beside Sam with his arm round her and her head on his shoulder, Ann said sleepily, "This is real isn't it?"

"Yes. It's real."

"It's strange. We seem to have spent ages with your parents. Yet, actually, since we met so much has happened in a very short time. It's like our personal fairytale. Time seems to behave oddly in those."

"Are we talking Grimm here?"

Ann gently butted his chin. "Don't be mean. All fairytales have their dark side. I know that it hasn't been easy lately. I'm sorry that we've been unkind to each other sometimes. But now we will live happily ever after."

"Yes, my beloved, we will. I just hope that you aren't always going to see our life in terms of literary genres. As we've agreed, this is real."

"I promise that the only book I'll consider relevant from now on will be Mrs. Beeton's Book of Household Management."

Sam looked down at her and bent over to kiss the tip of her nose. "That sounds a bit dull. How about something rather more interesting?" He kissed her neck. "Remember the erotic Indian texts I told you about the other day?"

He bent again and smothered her laughing face with kisses. "Yes. I see you do know the ones I mean. Well, why don't you forget about Mrs Beeton? Those would be much more exciting."

SEVEN

Ann had, in fact, never seen a copy of Mrs Beeton but, though merely a part of the literary landscape of her mind, the book suddenly became a metaphor for an ironic side effect of her romantic rebellion. Since meeting Sam, caught up in the combined stress and exhilaration of all that was happening to her, she had rarely looked beyond the moment. On her first morning alone in the flat, she was confronted by the mundane consequences of that blind, onward rush and brought face to face with unforeseen challenges. The domestic facts of life pressed in on her from every corner of these empty rooms. This unconstructed space had to be turned into a home. She and Sam had to be fed. Cleanliness and comfort would have to be created in routine battles against dirt and disorder. She, with all her inadequacies, was the person who would be responsible for all this.

"You must find good servants." Perin was soon on the scene to see that all was well. "You won't manage without them."

"I'll be alright for a month or so." Ann had regained her nerve and was anxious to hold onto the renewed bliss of being alone with Sam. "I only have to go downstairs and cross the street to find shops with all the basic necessities and everyone in them speaks English. Well, a kind of English.

And there's nothing to clean yet. The place is practically bare."

"The floors and bathrooms need to be done." Perin was firm. "Sam would feel bad to see you doing such jobs. I will send someone over each morning to do them until you get settled. I will also send over a few dishes each day for you to warm up so that Sam can have some of his favourite foods. Remember you are not used to working in this climate and, later, the monsoon will make everything difficult. Have your month. Then we will see what is to be done."

Ann was ruefully aware that she had been right about the impossibility of freedom but, knowing that eventually she would have to get to grips with employing some sort of help and finding the humidity exhausting, was secretly glad of Perin's next intervention.

"I know you want to wait, Ann, but I have found a servant for you. This is really a good chance. God is great. My sister's bearer – he's been with them for years and he's a diamond – has a cousin looking for work who has been for five years a cook-bearer. The people he was working for have gone abroad. You will really like him. These men come from a hill region in the north and they are noted for being loyal and hard working."

Ann did like him. Kishen Datt had something of the look of a Gurkha. He was short and stocky, with a round, cheerful face and she recognised in him a sturdy sense of self that, though he was polite and attentive, was never lost in the subservience that had often distressed her in Perin's servants. As a bonus, he would bring with him a young nephew who would do all their general cleaning – even the bathrooms. This was a relief to Ann who had found the constant visits of a special sweeper to do such work in Dahanipur House intrusive and inconvenient. She wanted to keep her own household simple, spare and self-contained.

She showed Kishen the rooms she intended for him.

"There is space for your wife here. Why don't you bring her to Bombay? I want you to be happy and comfortable with us."

"No, Memsahib. She is village girl. She needs to be with her family. She is unhappy and lonely in city."

Ann, who, even with all her advantages, missed her familiar support systems, the background faces and places that she had always taken for granted, saw very clearly what it would be like for a girl from an Indian village to have to cope with a similar loss. "Well, Kishen, we'll have to see that you get home to her for a long visit every year."

Hiring a servant was going much more smoothly than she had expected but her determination to give him three weeks' annual leave and the level of pay she felt it fair to offer him met with Perin's strong disapproval – and Sam wasn't completely on her side.

"This is a whole new thing for you to deal with and you should really listen to my mother. I'm quite happy about the pay you want to give. I like Kishen too. He's very suitable and I'm really glad that you've found someone you can get on with. It's absolutely true, though, that you will cause trouble all round by giving him more leave than my aunt gives her bearer. Don't forget that it's never a good idea to be too lenient or friendly."

"Sam, I can't believe that's what you really feel." She tried to ignore the slight dismay that any sign of his having an alien view of things caused in her. "Anyway, what experience have you had in managing servants? You're simply spouting the mantras that I keep hearing from your mother and her friends. We have to be generous. It's bad enough that the poor man has to live apart from his family. He should at least have enough time with them once a year. I have to do what I feel is right."

She knew that in finding Kishen she had been extremely lucky. She was walking a tightrope between the observances of Indian life and her western sensibilities, trying to keep her mother-in-law and the family happy while holding her own standards intact. Any hint of abstract priggishness in her attitude would be tempered by the obvious possibility of genuine affection and respect for this new person in her life, by the very fact, indeed, that this was how she viewed him.

By the end of April, both Kishen and his nephew, Ram Datt, had settled in. Sam was enjoying his job and had his own fixed timetable and Ann was, so far, managing to fill her days with the decoration and organisation of the flat. Two living rooms and two of the bedrooms were furnished and what was needed for the third bedroom, which was to be used as a study, had been ordered. In the evenings, they were out regularly, to parties, to cinemas and to the many concerts and plays on offer in the city. When they stayed in, they sat on their balcony, looking out over the sea and chatting casually about small things. Such tranquil interludes were like the slow-moving surface of a river, smoothly concealing a ferocious undertow fed by the surge of their shared exhilaration, the turbulence of daily living and the tug of conflicting loyalties; a force that whirled and eddied unseen around the deep, drowned wreckage of submerged tensions and grievances.

A large part of Sam's attention was necessarily focused on his work. Ann had no equivalent interest. The creative elements of setting up house were soon largely over and the chores of maintenance were carried out for her. She did not mind spending time alone, having always been somewhat solitary. It wasn't loneliness but lack of purpose that bothered her and, increasingly, after Sam left for the office, she felt restless and confined.

One morning in the first week of May, in just such a mood, she set out for central Bombay. On an earlier outing with Perin, she had seen some table linen that she now decided would be an ideal gift for her mother's birthday the following month. It would be easy to pack and post and she told herself that this was a matter of urgency. She felt a flutter of nervousness at the thought of venturing into the city on her own and the fierce pre-monsoon heat that hit her as she went out made her hesitate again, almost driving her back inside, but the idea of a morning spent in the flat, stifling in every way, hit her as forcefully and she flagged down a passing taxi.

She was sure that she knew exactly where the large shop she wanted was located and got down from the cab before reaching it, intending to walk the rest of the way and call in to one or two others as she went, partly to make her outing worthwhile and partly to test her ability to find her way around without help, but, after paying off the driver, she saw that she had miscalculated and that she had considerably further to go than she had anticipated. She struggled on through what seemed like a solid barrier of humid air, seared by horrifying flashes of rage as people in the jostling crowd on the pavement continually bumped against her. All her customary restraints seemed to have burned away and she felt a primitive urge to jab out with her elbows and really hurt someone. As she entered each shop, she met a palpable layer of musty heat and by the time that she reached the handicraft store she was looking for, she was exhausted and her legs were weak and trembling. She was hoping for some relief from its many high ceiling fans but as she opened the door and walked in, an exhalation of stored atmosphere washed over her as stale as bad breath. Her vision blurred and a spurt of nausea burned her throat.

"Come and sit down."

She was vaguely aware of a slender, feminine figure helping her to a chair and handing her a handkerchief soaked in cologne.

"Here! Wipe your forehead with this."

"Thank you." She tried to sit straight. "I'll be alright in a minute. I just need to get a taxi and go home."

"Don't do that. You look *so* ill. My car and driver are right outside. Come to my flat and cool down. When you feel better, you can explain how we can get you back. Don't worry. I'm not a kidnapper. My husband, Bob, belongs to the British High Commission and he's the most respectable man in Bombay – if not India."

A further wash of salt liquid scoured Ann's mouth leaving her shaky and insubstantial, incapable of decision or protest and this light, confident, English voice was immensely reassuring. She allowed herself to be led outside and, after a short drive, taken up into a large, air-conditioned room. In the sudden cold, like a wilted flower given water, she unfolded, straightened and revived. She was given an iced lime juice. Her head cleared and for the first time she looked directly at her rescuer. Blue eyes smiled back from a small, animated face framed by a dark, beautifully cut bob.

"Oh good. You're much better. Now I can introduce myself. I'm Jessica Clark. Jess."

"I'm Ann Mehta."

"But you're English aren't you?"

"Yes but my husband, Sam, is Indian."

"How thrilling! You must tell me all about him. Look Ann, today I'll be having lunch by myself. I desperately need company. It is *so* lucky that I have met you. Do you have to get back soon? Couldn't you stay and go later? Do. Please. I'll be your friend forever."

Such extravagant language broke all the rules for Ann and previously she would have hastily retreated, but she had travelled further from home than the nautical miles that she had covered and replied warmly and simply. "I do need a friend. I'd like to stay."

Though they were alone, a cold lunch was formally served and looking across the table at Jess and seeing features that spoke of home, she was once more aware of the gap left in her life by the loss of familiar faces and voices and found herself talking like a prisoner emerging from solitary confinement, expressing feelings that, until now, she had hardly allowed herself to acknowledge.

"Has absolutely everyone you've met asked you how you like their country?" Jess pulled a wry face. "How *do* you like it, Ann? Oh! That's probably tactless. It's now your country too."

"Actually, it's only a colourful backdrop to my life. I've no real sense of it yet as *a* country, let alone *my* country. I'm not sure that it will ever be that. Can you change your deepest feelings about where you really belong?"

"I don't have to deal with that question of course but I love it. The one drawback is finding things a bit claustrophobic among the people we mix with. They have rather a lot of stuffy rules. I'm *so* pleased to have met you. You are getting to know the real India."

"I haven't seen that much of it, actually. I haven't been outside Bombay yet or even that far afield in the city itself. I go out with Sam and his family but rarely anywhere on my own. I move about well enough in the area around our building and use the shops there but look what a mess I've made of this foray out alone. If I go on like this, I'll never know it properly."

"Are you coping with the language? Bob's set up lessons for me but I don't really find I need it."

"I'm having lessons too, but it's not the spoken language I need to learn. It's the unspoken one. You know – the things that in England you never have to be told, that never have to be spelled out because they are so much a part of you. Here I sometimes feel that I'm walking about blindfolded, blundering into things. Before this, my life was so slow. Nothing ever happened to me. Then I was caught up in a tornado and whirled away. It's certainly exciting."

"Do you find being married as exciting as you expected it to be?"

Ann looked thoughtfully at Jess. "I hadn't any ideas about it. Perhaps I was weird. I was a complete innocent, so what happened with Sam was overwhelming but it happened to him too and I don't think it would be right to discuss it with anyone else."

"I didn't mean to pry. I wanted to talk about it myself. It's wonderful, of course, and I adore Bob but I do miss my parents. I didn't expect to. Their life together always seemed to me like a long private conversation in the background that I never really listened to but now I feel an odd sort of silence. Bob is very matter of fact. He doesn't discuss things. He does them. Of course that's why I wanted him. He takes care of all the boring bits of life and just lets me live it."

There was an awkward pause. Ann felt a need to mark a boundary. Bob, like Sam, deserved his privacy. Anxious not to seem censorious, she hastily began to talk about other things and found herself telling Jess about her reactions to the distressing sights that affronted her daily. Sam understood how upsetting these were but having lived with the surrounding deprivation all his life, had necessarily come to terms with it. Jess must feel as she did.

"I'm ashamed at how often I can't look directly at beggars. They are people with feelings. It's not good enough to simply give them money, practically throw it at them and rush away." She hesitated. "I'm a hypocrite, Jess. I can't tell you how staid, well dull, my life was at home and I'd be lying if I said I don't enjoy the way things are for me here. I'm fast adapting to parties, glamorous clothes, jewelry and servants. Then I have awful moments when I think of all that misery. Do you think that we are parasites?"

Jess looked outraged. "No! We can't be held responsible for the geography and history that cause all this and it wouldn't make it any better if we stopped having things. Someone produces the clothes and jewelry you talk about and earns money that way. That's true of everything we use."

"That sounds so rational but it somehow doesn't entirely convince me. My doubts don't stop me looking forward to my next party though."

Two days later Jess came to visit Ann for the first time and was enchanted with her flat.

"Ann! It's gorgeous. Mine suddenly seems *so* boring. I thought that white was *the* colour to combat heat but it isn't very interesting and I feel I have to fill every room with masses of flowers to brighten things up. I spend hours arranging them. This is *so* wonderful. It's like woodland and water."

Ann had chosen a pale, mossy green for all the walls, ceilings and paintwork and grouped palms and large potted plants in the corners of the rooms. The effect was cool and restful and she was very pleased with it and with herself for displaying unexpected skills.

"And I love the furniture. What is it? I can only describe it as blonde. It's *so* light. It seems to float. What a triumph!"

"It's bleached teak. Sam was a bit dubious about it although he likes it now. He was used to a very different style. So was I. I love my parents' cottage but it was nothing like this. I do feel I've made it both livable and elegant. Have you seen many Indian homes?"

"Not really. We seem to have met all our local friends in public places so far."

"Well, I shouldn't be hyper-critical but I haven't seen one I'd like to live in. Some of them have what I can only call a ramshackle splendor. They have huge rooms and lovely antiques but a rather dusty and uncoordinated effect. Then there are those where the public rooms are very grand with carved furniture and chandeliers but the private rooms are often rather bleak, utterly utilitarian with strip lights and steel cupboards."

"They don't sound very comfortable."

"Well, comfort is a difficult concept to transplant. At home it means warm, closed spaces, squishy chairs and plump cushions. That's what I miss sometimes but it's not suitable here."

"I'm sure that it's your family rather than a familiar décor that you miss. How often do you hear from them?"

"Mother writes every week but my father never answers my letters or comments on anything I write about. He can't forgive me for leaving them."

"Ann! You know that it is always the women of the family who make the effort at keeping contact. You shouldn't read too much into that."

"I'm afraid it's true, Jess. He's always been interested in every possible subject, always eager to learn something new, but he ignores India and anything I tell them about it and he doesn't respond to any suggestion that they should come here and see it for themselves. I've really hurt him and he can't get over it."

"Obviously it is difficult for him to lose you. You must give him more time. He will soon look forward to coming here. Couldn't you go home for a visit?"

Ann's face clouded. "You know how people can be about foreigners in England. My parents were so worried about what our family and friends think of me and what I've done that they've made me nervous about seeing them all again. But it's not just that. I'm afraid that going back would unsettle and confuse me. There are times when I think about home and ache for it. I wouldn't say this to anyone else but I daren't go back. Not yet. Not till I feel more secure here."

Jess hugged her. "I'm sure that everyone wants you to be happy and no one thinks badly of you. How could they? You will go home again and your family will visit you. Everyone will realise how right this is for you. Everything will be fine."

Jess met Ann's need for someone with whom to share the days and offered understanding and agreeable company. They met almost daily and they soon knew as much about each other's lives as if they had been friends from childhood. At first, Sam viewed this friendship with misgiving. Since their arrival in India his worries about separating Ann from her own world had been overtaken by a need to see her integrated into his. She seemed less homesick than he had expected her to be and he decided that the challenges she faced demanded so large a part of her energies that there was no time left for any nostalgia. All her thoughts appeared to be concentrated on her new life. He felt that Jess, sharing attitudes and memories with her that he had no part in, posed a threat to that single-mindedness but his introduction to Bob somewhat allayed these fears. They felt an instant rapport. Sam found Bob's enthusiasm for the country he was assigned to engaging and impressive and he was given a new take on the intimacy between Ann and Jess.

"Meeting Ann has been good for Jess, Sam. Of course I'm pleased that they have each other, given that they must both miss England and their families but it's also great that Jess has a chance to have closer contact with India through getting to know you both. I don't want her to become a typical ex-pat."

"I can't somehow see Jess as a Memsahib."

"No, Jess doesn't fit easily into any category." Bob looked fondly across at his wife. "She mostly goes her own way."

Soon, they were spending any evenings free of social commitments at each other's homes and while Sam and

Bob had long serious conversations, Ann and Jess shared their secrets like schoolgirls together, rather as if they were enjoying the special intimacy that neither of them had ever actually had at school, Ann being too solitary and Jess too generally popular for such closeness.

"My mother-in-law is a bit of a trial." Jess received regular letters from Bob's mother. "She's like a grand and granite mountain. Very craggy and mostly shrouded in fog. The sun only comes out when Bob's around. I'm clearly not good enough for him. You seem to get on very well with yours. It's supposed to be a fraught relationship for anyone and considering that you've snatched her son not only from her but from their very close community you'd think it would be lethal for you."

"I have to hand it to Perin. There are moments when we could upset each other but she's very sensible. The only annoying thing about her is her obsession with my reproductive powers. Do you know that within hours of my arrival she was seeing herself as a grandmother! If Sam had any children, even with me, they would be considered Parsis and that is important to her. I think it's when their girls marry outsiders that the children are lost to them but I haven't asked many questions. There is so much to deal with and I don't make any serious effort to be part of it all"

"But you try so hard, Ann. You see all Sam's family only too often. You're there for all their important occasions. You wear saris to their parties. You try to give Sam all his familiar food. You never do anything that would offend them."

"That's all superficial. Eating curry and wearing a sari doesn't turn you into someone else. In a way it gives a false impression. Like wearing fancy dress. Pretending to be something you aren't. I've not really learnt much about their religion and sometimes I feel that they think about things in ways I don't begin to understand. Just getting through the small problems of daily living seems enough to cope with for now and it's much easier to drift across the surface of it all. Sam seems torn between wanting me to behave more like them and a sort of perverse pride in my being different. He often seems determined that we should not be pulled into family, religion and community ways. We have to be careful or what will we actually end up as? Displaced people? Belonging nowhere?" Her eyes clouded and she said abruptly, "Have you ever thought about having children, Jess?"

There was no answer and a most extraordinary expression passed over her friend's face. It struck Ann that Jess was completely floored by the idea of herself as a parent, that in her mind she was still the centre of a continuing golden girlhood. A cool breath passed over their friendship. She had recently been aware of an astringency in her character that had surprised her. These days she was looking at life and the people she met with a very sharp eye. To a degree this was a mode of self-defence, for circumstances had turned her into an outsider, subject to a curiosity that, on the whole friendly, could occasionally be felt as hostile scrutiny and she was responding by becoming colder and more critical herself. Now, she was even being unfair to her dearest friend for, like Jess, she had never thought of herself as a mother. Sam was completely relaxed about the rather feverish atmosphere surrounding them.

"Eventually it would be good to have children but for now I only want you. This obsession with 'Good News' is an age old thing. We can forget all that."

She remembered his comment that their wedding would not be the usual joyful occasion. What about the births of their children? If she sensed any misgivings about foreign grandchildren on either side of the Indian-English divide would she be capable of unselfconscious motherhood?

"Ann." She was recalled by Jess touching her shoulder. "Ann, don't agonize. Don't take everything so hard. Don't let anyone tell you how to live your life. Sam is *so* beautiful and he loves you. Enjoy that. Have fun together. Look! One of Bob's Indian friends is lending us his seaside bungalow at Mahu this weekend. It seems that he hardly uses it. Come with us. Forget the family lunch. You and Sam can get right away from it all. We'll have a wonderful time."

Ann's momentary aloofness melted away. She knew that many Bombayites had beach houses at places like Mahu, along the coast north of the city, and that many companies owned such holiday chalets for the use of their staff.

"I'd love to. I'm sure that Sam would too. I'll let you know."

When she told Sam about this invitation, he firmly suppressed a harsh thought. Their stay in Dahanipur House had shown him how easily even the slightest flaw in a relationship could be exacerbated by the pressures and proximity of other people. They wouldn't be taking any servants with them on this trip. It would be just the four of them, alone together for two uninterrupted days in a small bungalow, with no outside distractions. Even though they all got on well, this would take their friendship to a new level and could possibly change it in ways they hadn't imagined. He looked at Ann's eager face. Of course they would go. She deserved a break.

"It sounds good. I went to Mahu once or twice with friends before going to England. It's totally undeveloped and very peaceful. Quite idyllic really."

EIGHT

They set off very early on Saturday morning. Leaving Bombay meant a lengthy and exhausting journey through miles of increasingly decrepit suburbs whose tumultuous life continually flowed onto and across the narrow road with all the chaotic but instinctively purposeful drive of a swarm of bees round a hive. The car shouldered its way through this ferment of people and animals that only gradually thinned and quietened, until, at last, they rounded the final bend of the increasingly bumpy road and were engulfed in an endless and empty wash of blue, where a cloudless sky melted into a wide bay and their ears rang with the unfamiliar silence.

They drove cautiously down onto a gravel track that followed the curve of the shoreline and, passing two substantial holiday houses and a long stretch of sandy, tussocky grass, drew up on a wide, weedy patch in front of a low building set back within a shady garden.

"Oh dear!" Looking ruefully at this, with its narrow, uneven verandah and peeling paint, Bob got slowly out of the car. "I think my friend was overstating things a bit. To call it a bungalow is stretching it. Shack seems like a more accurate description. I can see why he rarely uses this place."

"I think it's cute." Jess had leapt out of the car and opened a small white gate. She ran up the path, climbed some wooden steps to the verandah and peered in through a dusty window next to the central door. "Come on, Bob. Bring the keys. I want to see inside."

They went into a dimly lit hall-cum-living room. At the far end, a rather battered door, hung with a bamboo curtain, led into a simple kitchen and on either side wall, a smaller, unevenly painted one opened into a double bedroom with an attached bathroom. Like the kitchen, these washrooms were very basic, each one a white tiled space with a toilet and basin at one end and a utilitarian metal showerhead set in the ceiling at the other.

"I'm sorry, Sam." Bob was still apologetic. "I should have checked it out before asking you to come with us."

"Oh, Bob!" Jess sounded impatient. "It's perfect. We don't want anything to look after or feel responsible for. There's certainly nothing here we could spoil and the garden is heavenly."

"Everything is fine, Bob," Ann said calmly. "All we need is a bed and a shower. What we've come for is peace, and Jess is right. The garden's lovely and the beach is beautiful."

The garden was certainly the most attractive feature of the place, a cool refuge with a table and an assortment of garden chairs set out invitingly in the deep shade of huge hibiscus shrubs, coconut palms and other tall trees while, beyond the gate and across the track, the beach glittered blindingly in the sunlight.

"The beach may look beautiful but pretty soon that sand will probably burn the soles off our feet," Bob said. "Let's unload the car quickly and bathe while it's still bearable."

All the perishables were packed in large ice boxes, so, stacking these in the kitchen, they left everything to be organised later, simply opening their suitcases and changing into their swimwear, before running down to the sea.

Sam and Bob were strong swimmers and raced each other out into the bay. Jess and Ann were less confident and swam gently in parallel with the shore for a while before coming back to sit on the sand, leaning back on their elbows and letting the waves break over their legs. They watched the two heads moving further and further away.

"They are rather far out." Jess sounded anxious. "They haven't swum here before. It's a bit reckless. It looks like male rivalry to me."

She stood up, waving and calling and, when at last the men turned and headed back towards them, Ann, too, got to her feet. They stood side by side, Ann straight and sturdy in a plain black swimsuit, Jess rounded and feminine in a red two-piece. Reaching the shallows ahead of Bob, Sam could not help staring at her. She had always appeared slight and girlish to him but a flush of excitement shocked him at this unexpected view of her. Then Bob came up out of the water and Jess rushed over to him, put her arms round his waist and her head on his chest. Sam looked away and went over to Ann.

"Well, that was something," she said with raised brows.

"What was?" Sam sounded uneasy.

"Seeing Jess in a state. I've never known her to worry about anything before. I've never seen her concerned about Bob either. She usually seems to think he is capable of dealing with anything, that nothing can touch him. She was afraid that an element of competitiveness was driving you both to take risks."

"We were fine." Sam's voice was suddenly jaunty. "There was absolutely nothing to worry about. The bay is like a pond."

"All that effort has made me hungry." Bob came over to them, holding Jess's hand. "Let's find out how good you two pampered girls are in the kitchen. Or have you forgotten how a kitchen works?"

"We neither of us ever really knew that." Ann smiled at him. "You can't blame India for our ignorance. But we are both smart girls. I'm sure we will manage to feed you."

There was, in fact, no cooking to do as their servants had prepared and packed cold food for this first meal and, while Bob and Sam found and opened bottles of chilled beer, Ann and Jess dished it up and carried it outside. It was a long, leisurely meal and after reluctantly rousing themselves to the unaccustomed chore of clearing away and washing the dishes, they came back into the garden and sat chatting idly. The heat and humidity, the sound of the waves and the whisper of the breeze in the trees above them made them slow and drowsy but after an hour or so, Jess stood up.

"I'm going for a walk. Anyone coming?"

"It's so hot," said Ann. "I don't know if I can after all that food."

"Take it easy, Jess, we can go later. There's no rush." Bob settled more comfortably into his chair.

"No. I'm feeling restless. I want to go now. If you are all too bloated to move, I'll go alone."

"I'll come." Sam eased out of his recliner.

As the two of them walked towards the shore and he bent down to Jess, laughing at some unheard comment, Ann felt a painful tightness in her chest. How beautiful they were! Side by side they seemed to have an enhanced brilliance that caught one's breath.

Bob saw her face. "Perhaps we're being lazy. I think we should go too. Let's follow them."

He shouted out to the others, "Hi! We're coming after all."

Sam turned with a smile. "It's not so hot. We can take it slowly." He held out his hand to Ann and her momentary discomfort vanished.

Jess was still facing straight ahead, ignoring them all. "Well I need some real exercise." She now looked at Bob. "If you're coming, you'll have to speed up." She set off at an exaggerated pace and he took long strides to catch up with her.

"I'm glad you changed your mind. I didn't like to think of Jess going off on her own," Sam stroked Ann's palm with one finger, "but she can be rather wearing and Bob can deal with that. We don't need to be so athletic. We'll only go as far as those rocks along there and wait for them to come back to us."

When they reached the rocks they sat on a smooth boulder and Sam put his arm round Ann and pulled her close. She was sharply aware of the sticky, salty heat of his skin and leant her head on his shoulder. In contented silence they watched as Bob and Jess dwindled into the distance and then disappeared beyond a slight rise, where a raised finger of sand pointed out to sea, defining the left hand curve of the bay. A similar narrow spit of land marked its right hand curve more vigorously, running out into the water through a spiky jangle of rocks and spray. In the distance beyond this was a misty shoreline punctuated with palms. Far out, three rounded islets paddled like plump matrons in the faintly rippled surface of the water. Everything floated in a dreamlike, gauzy haze. This was India leached of its vivid violence – sensual and soporific.

They all grew increasingly heavy-limbed and light-headed. Though they swam once more just before sunset and again early the next morning, they could then only just summon the energy to prepare food, spending all their time lazing in the garden. They had no planned entertainments. Bob and Sam started a game of chess. Ann selected a rather sandy paperback from among a tattered pile in a cupboard indoors and Jess flipped through some equally tattered and somewhat out-of-date magazines. All too quickly, given these desultory occupations, it was time to rouse themselves and fight their way home through the suburbs, promising to arrange another such trip as soon as possible.

Soon after this, Bob was offered a chance to rent the house on a regular and fixed term basis. He was not one to rush into anything without being sure of his ground and talked it over with the others.

"Are you quite sure that you do all like the place? It's very small and hardly luxurious. We could find something better if you'd prefer to."

"Bob! Don't talk about it like that. It already feels like ours. We love it." Jess caught Ann's hand. "You love it. Don't you?"

"I think that its being small is a positive advantage." Sam, like Bob, was considering practicalities. "Most people with beach houses suddenly find they have more friends than they had realised. The whole point is to escape and be peaceful. There won't be that many people who would share our feelings about such a simple place and if they did, we can simply say that there isn't room to accommodate them."

So Bob signed a long lease that made the bungalow available to them whenever they could get away, even at short notice, and throughout the rest of that year, these agreeable weekends were as frequent as they could make them. Each time they went, Ann felt that she was coming to a place like many that she had cherished throughout her childhood; places where on arrival she would rush out to check their well-loved features. Here, she always wanted to see a deep rock pool, the boulder that provided a viewpoint over the distant coastline, a small ruined tower beyond the rise. Such things were comforting fixtures in the challenging precariousness of life and made this a refuge where she found something of the unchanging slowness of her old home.

In the city, not only did they dash from activity to activity amidst constant noise, they were, paradoxically, tied down in all sorts of ways. They each had their allotted personal and official slots within a much categorized system. Bob and Jess had defined duties within a rigid social calendar and Sam and Ann were committed to functions related to Sam's work and to numerous family occasions in a way that mocked all they had expected when they came together in such an apparently radical way. While servants made their lives much easier on a practical level, they also imposed additional obligations and fixed modes of behaviour on them. At Mahu, they cast all this aside. It became very special for them. Alone with the sea, the sky, the beach and each other, they were temporarily free of such impositions and restrictions and here, their friendship, like that of children, was a coming together of their natural selves.

Meanwhile, in Bombay, they were creating a second agreeable meeting place among a set of young friends brought together from both sides. It was a bright, cosmopolitan crowd and though its numbers increased, diminished and grew again, shaped by the restless mobility of its members, a steady nucleus persisted through all these changes. For Sam and Bob, this was a rewarding way to spend time with colleagues and business contacts. For Ann, meeting so many amusing and articulate people, all working in diverse fields, was a pleasure that she could never have experienced in rural England. Jess, popular and indulged by everyone, was usually the centre of some lively group but was more and more inclined to gravitate towards one particular girl. Sarla Patel, an editor of one of Bombay's magazines, was very like her, spirited and self-possessed and seeing these two magnetic creatures together caused Ann some pangs of jealousy but she was distracted by finding herself increasingly sought out by one of Sam's business contacts.

Harilal Chand, Hari as they all called him, was a young Hindu, broad-shouldered and stocky, with a clever, pockmarked face. He was not at all good-looking but there was something about him that fascinated her and, no longer physically naïve, she was very aware of a spark between them. Half ashamed of feeling any such interest beyond her much defended commitment to Sam, she felt a marked excitement when they were together and, in spite of herself, flirting was a natural and irresistible response. Hari was, moreover, interesting and knowledgeable, with a worthwhile opinion on most subjects and she soon tested him on her ongoing dilemma.

"Do you ever think of us as parasites?"

He gave her a serious look. "I don't but I can see how you might be troubled by our comforts when you compare them to the apocalyptic miseries around us. The reality is that demand for such comforts will be an engine for progress. We are all well off but we aren't the rich of India. We're the top end of a middle class. The growth of an even larger middle class will mean a breakthrough for this country. I don't know if we will see it happen."

"I'm too ignorant to have a view on that. I still know very little about the politics and economics of India. I'm only able to see things as a personal problem and I'm horrified to find that, constantly exposed to pain and poverty, I seem to be getting hardened to it. My excuse is that this may be the only way that I can deal with it. Like doctors or nurses who couldn't function if they allowed themselves to be overwhelmed by the sight of suffering."

"So? Why did you put yourself through all this?"

"Love." Ann looked straight at him.

He grinned at her. "Love is just a construct. And a Western construct at that. Of course Parsis like Sam are so modern and enlightened that they are adopting it too. Even some Hindus are beginning to take it up, but we have no ingrained belief in it and without that belief it has no power. We're lucky. Our lives aren't generally shaped by this abstraction. Our marriages are usually purely practical and, as a result, successful." He flushed and looked horrified. "I'm sorry. I'm letting my tongue run away with me. I didn't mean to be personal. I'm sometimes too clever for my own good and forget what I'm actually saying."

"Well you may have *some* truth on your side. I suppose there has to be a strong element of practicality in any socially recognised relationship. I know only too well how emotions, all kinds of emotions, can confuse the issue. But whatever you say, love certainly feels to me like more than some intellectual idea." She hesitated for a moment. "Perhaps you just haven't been struck down yet. Then again, perhaps you are a protected species."

Hari took her hand. "Ann, I have to say that I don't feel protected right now. In fact I feel distinctly endangered."

Aware of flirting not only with him but with disloyalty, she firmly removed her hand. "You are a tease Hari. I'm sorry I bothered you with my over-refined conscience but it's always useful to hear what you think. Now! Let's go and find Sam."

Later, getting ready for bed, she said, "Sam, what do you think of Hari? Do you like him?"

He gave her a considering look. "He's a good businessman. The company find him a useful supplier. Reliable and conscientious. Very bright."

"He can be frighteningly clever. He was telling me that he sees a growing middle class as India's salvation. I said that I wasn't knowledgeable enough to comment. What do you think?"

Sam sat on a chair and began unlacing his shoes. "I think you are a great deal more knowledgeable than you pretend my dearest girl. You are very clever too. I'm quite sure that Hari doesn't actually intimidate you."

Ann moved behind him and bending down, cradled his head, rubbing her face in his hair and inhaling its familiar and distinctive scent. "I do love you Sam."

He pulled her round beside him and onto his knee. "So do I."

It was one of the silly jokes that are part of the glue holding marriages together. She resolved to give up dangerous talks with Hari but could not resist asking Jess what she thought of him.

"He can be fun but he's rather ugly. I know that I'm being shallow and that it shouldn't matter but I like people to look good."

"Being attractive isn't always a question of appearance. I find him rather intriguing actually."

"Ann! How can you even think like that about him? You've got Sam and he's the most beautiful man I know."

"Well you've got Bob. Why are you rating Sam so highly?" Ann's tone was somewhat sharp.

"Of course Bob is my prop and stay, so tall and solid that I always long to lean on him. He's very presentable, but everyone can see that Sam is gorgeous and, amazingly, that he doesn't seem to know that he is."

Ann decided to accept this as an aesthetic judgment. She knew that Jess was extremely fond of Sam but they were all four bound together by a deep affection. She and Sam considered Bob a special friend, warmly appreciating his good sense and, while Sam could be critical of Jess in her more demanding moods, he admitted her charm and they both understood only too well how much harder Ann's life would be without such a compatible and understanding companion. For, in spite of all these diversions and her new friends, she was still fretted by a sense of aimlessness. This was one of the few things she did not talk over with Jess and something she was wary of discussing with Sam. Occasionally, she wondered whether, for all that his time abroad had opened him to, Sam was more tied to an oriental view of a wife's place in her husband's life than he would admit. She was treading carefully in delicate areas, avoiding unsettling confrontations. She was also avoiding difficult thoughts about her parents. That was another problem best postponed until she was truly settled into this new life. It was increasingly a relief to get away to Mahu, to lie back and soak up the sun, forget it all and enjoy a few hours of tranquility, lulled by the gentle sounds of the wind and the sea.

NINE

Sam had been powerless to resist his need to bring Ann to India though wrung by a sense of his selfishness in doing so. He could not shake off disturbing thoughts of the continuing rift with his in-laws. It seemed to him unforgivable that his intentions of building bridges between Ann's relations and himself had come to nothing but he understood her dread of their reactions to him – the material evidence of her supposed misjudgement – and he could not bring himself to force the issue. Most weeks, she received a stiff little letter from her mother and it was plain that, even after the trauma of their separation, life in Norfolk continued almost unchanged and at the same slow pace. These letters always included messages that were supposedly from her father. This was clearly not true. He still did not have anything to say to her. The question of their seeing each other again was on hold. Being apart was painful but the thought of being together was equally so.

If this was a nagging worry for Sam, he had other more immediate issues of his own. He was constantly under pressure to make hard choices between old habits and those required by his new responsibilities. Though Ann was confronting a strange and challenging world, it was one that, notwithstanding headaches and heartaches, stimulated and rewarded her and her break with her past had of necessity been clear and clean. His was long drawn out and tortuous. He was surrounded by places and people that were part of his boyhood and proximity to his parents made it harder to make changes or to demonstrate where his loyalties now lay. His work and time at the office helped. These were productive hours in which he acquired a separate character as a member of a team of professionals who valued his individuality, respected his opinions and confirmed his adult worth.

His leisure time too was invigorating. The intimacy with Jess and Bob was, at its best, like a desired version of family solidarity, offering affection, understanding and support and within their wider circle, admiration and liking were hard won but satisfying. He saw Ann, creatively fulfilled in her home, on acceptable working terms with his parents, resting on her friendship with Jess, display a growing social confidence and he was on the whole less constrained, less watchful of her moods and his own motivations.

Another year passed with little change and at surprising speed, with many of their problems seemingly tamed and tractable. Though Zal still checked them over from time to time, always drawing Sam aside into his room for a private talk on financial matters before their frequent Sunday lunches at Dahanipur House, he was almost convinced that Sam was a responsible householder. Perin, an amenable mother-in-law, had nevertheless been conditioned to see it as her duty to ensure that her son was properly cared for. Though she rarely commented on Ann's arrangements, she obviously kept them under close scrutiny. Luckily, having been instrumental in installing Kishen she was predisposed in his favour and had few faults to find.

Sam was often preoccupied with his work, needing to concentrate on his developing career, but he made it clear that he was far more aware of her frustrations than Ann had allowed.

"I can see that you are restless. I was thinking that it might be a good idea for you to start giving tuitions at home."

She was surprised and uncertain. "What sort of tuitions?"

"Conversation classes. There are many foreigners working around the city who speak the language but feel a need to refine their use of it. You could help them. I think you'd find it worthwhile. It wouldn't be like teaching children. It should be stimulating and you'd meet new and interesting people."

"But I have no teaching qualifications."

"You've got your A- levels and you wouldn't be setting yourself up as a teacher but offering speaking practice. As an Englishwoman you would have special credibility. I think that it would be an ideal thing for you."

Ann rushed over to him and gave him a hug. "Sam, I don't appreciate you as I should. I'm unfair to you. I'm sorry that I'm sometimes disagreeable."

He held her closely. "I'll forgive you. You often have good reason to be upset. Don't think that I ever forget how trying it can be for you here and yet you always manage to make me happy. I know that can't be the sole purpose of your life but it's a great contribution to mine."

Ann nuzzled into his neck but he tilted her head back and planted feathery kisses all over her face. They stayed close for a long moment, every irritation forgotten.

Through their varied connections she soon built up a group of students and they did, indeed, enrich her life. Regular tutorials added structure to her days and she and Sam were now out almost every evening, enjoying plays, concerts, the cinema and a busy round of dinner parties which involved them in the giving of reciprocal dinners at home. Evenings together on their balcony, spent in quiet contemplation of the sea and gentle conversation, became a rarity but they experienced moments of quiet satisfaction. They were settled. They were strong. They were safe. The wound of their distance, physical and emotional, from Ann's family still festered but subconsciously they had never seen it as incurable. It was their final challenge. They would deal with it.

Jess had been told more about Ann's hidden resentments, fears and worries than anyone.

"I think my older relatives even see people from other parts of England as foreigners, never mind people from another country." Ann had sounded resigned.

"I can see that in your small town, where everyone knows everyone else, attitudes could be a bit backward. It's definitely not like that in Oxford and surely it wasn't in Cambridge."

"Well, no-one ever said anything but some people did give us sideways looks sometimes. I doubt if in England you ever see the open racism of segregation or apartheid. It's more insidious than that." Ann's voice was sad rather than angry. "What you constantly come up against is a pervasive, ingrained self-satisfaction. It's that unspoken language again." Her tone hardened. "People don't say it aloud but they might as well, 'We are so lucky to be English. We can only view everyone else with a patronising pity.' There's something wrong when friendships with foreigners can be collected like Boy Scout badges and even liberals, who fraternise on principle, can become a little hectic in their friendships with Asians and Africans."

"Be fair." Jess protested. "This isn't totally one-sided. Your in-laws weren't that thrilled when Sam married you."

"Not because they thought I was some lesser mortal. Their community is facing declining numbers and I wasn't a Parsi. For them it's a simple matter of fighting for survival."

"Perhaps there is an element of that with the English. We're an endangered species in a sense. We are finished as lords of the universe and subconsciously many people are clinging on to the feelings that went with that. They are also going down fighting."

"I don't know. It's all extremely hurtful." Ann closed her eyes for a moment. "Sam to me is just a human being, a person I love. It's horrible to have that tainted by all this. My feelings about everyone are under pressure. I hate being so anxious and twisted."

"Would you like me to get in touch with your parents while I'm on leave in England? Surely they would be happy to get some first-hand news of you. I could visit them if you like. Take presents if you want to send any."

"I'd rather you didn't. I'd rather wait to make any real contact until they are genuinely ready for it."

Jess was disappointed and found it hard to keep her feelings in check but knowing how entrenched this standoff had become and what a struggle it was for Ann to break free of it, she did not for once voice her own views and nothing further was said or done on that occasion, but as they were about to fly out for another leave in June 1968, both she and Bob broached the subject.

"We don't want to upset you," Jess put her arm round Ann's shoulder, "but we are still ready to visit your parents. You know that you are miserable about the way things are between you and I worry about Sam in all this. I'm sure he must be hurt to think that you are ashame......."

"Jess!" Bob cut in sharply. "Sam's feelings aren't a matter for speculation." He turned to Ann. "It's none of our business, of course, but we only want to help. Don't you think it might be a good thing for your father and mother to meet some flesh and blood friends from your world here? India must seem so far away and unreal to them. Meeting us might bring it closer; make it all more normal somehow."

"It probably would." Ann felt the force of what he had said. "No, Bob. Not probably. It definitely would." There were times when she herself had no clear sense of this country, when it was more an exotic background to her life than an integral part of it. How could her parents picture what it was like? She sighed deeply. "You are dears to want to do it but I have to sort this out myself. Don't worry about what Jess said, Bob. I do know how unfair this is on Sam. He should have got to know all my family from the start. You know how patriarchal things are here. Sam doesn't complain but I know that he is especially concerned about having had so little contact with my father. I have been cowardly. I've treated them all badly. I will deal with it, I promise you. I'll try again to get them to visit us."

"Perhaps you should both go there first," Bob said tentatively. "They might find it hard to come here while things are still unsettled between you. It is a long way from all they are used to. If they already knew Sam better it would be far less daunting."

Ann sighed again and put her hand on his arm. "I know you're right. Of course I do. Look! We'll try to go for Christmas. It's the time of year for reunions, a time when the whole family gets together. Sam would meet them all in a festive setting and that would make it much easier for everyone. I'll talk to him about getting time off. We still have about six months to arrange it. I promise that I'll write this week and ask my mother if it's alright with her."

Jess and Bob were relieved that Ann had at last made a definite decision and were sure that now she had made a promise she would keep it. She and Sam would be very much happier. After too much pain this might finally end well.

Sam was delighted by her change of heart. "It will be such a relief to get to see your parents at last. It's really been a huge weight on my mind and I've been especially concerned about you and feeling guilty for cutting you off from them like this. I can take three weeks leave in December. I'll start looking at travel arrangements. Commit you before you change your mind."

Ann still found it hard to get round to sending the necessary letter home. All this time, she and her mother had exchanged what amounted to dry catalogues of the surface events of their lives. They had not truly communicated for so long that she felt weighed down by an ingrown inertia. It would take such an effort to get back to natural ways of dealing with each other. Every day she intended to write and every day she put off doing so. She knew that she must pull herself together. It seemed incredible, but she had been here almost three years. Time was again playing its tricks. She had to see things more realistically. She did not have forever to sort things out.

TEN

One night, coming back late from a tiring, formal dinner party, Sam and Ann went straight out onto the balcony. Although Ann had told Kishen that he need not wait up when they ate out, he invariably opened the door to them no matter what hour they returned and, on this occasion, Sam asked him to bring them cold drinks. Though it was after midnight, it was still hot and heavy and they were dry-mouthed and sluggish after their drive home. Ann slipped off her shoes and sat with her face tilted up to the slight movement of air coming off the sea. Sam removed his jacket and was also about to sit down when the phone rang and she was still turned into the breeze with her eyes closed when he came back from taking the call.

"Whoever was that at this time?" Her voice was sleepy and casual.

There was no answer and she opened her eyes to see Sam standing beside her with a stricken look on his face.

"What is it? Who was that?"

"Ann, I have some bad news. That was your grandfather Fincham. Your father......."

"He's ill." Ann jumped up. "No! He's never ill."

"Dearest," Sam drew her to him. "It really is terrible news. Your father had a heart attack a short while ago." He held her closer. "Nothing could be done to save him."

She pulled away from him. "No! It can't be true. He's so healthy. He's so strong. It isn't true."

Sam came close and tried to put his arms around her but she pushed him away with a hostile look. "Don't. What have we done? Don't touch me." She leaned back against the balustrade, with her arms tightly folded, her face stony.

"Come inside. Come sweetheart." He gently guided her in. Kishen had brought their drinks but seeing that something was terribly wrong had waited by the balcony door. He stood aside, his normally bright face clouded with worry.

"Bring hot tea for Memsahib. Put lots of sugar in it."

Once indoors, Ann forgot her anger and rested against Sam, trembling but tearless.

"I should have spoken to grandpa. I should have talked to Mother."

"I think your grandfather would have found it distressing to talk to you. He seemed relieved that I answered the phone. Your mother wasn't with him. He was still at the cottage but she had gone back to the farm with your grandmother. I told him that we would arrange for you to go home immediately and that you would call tomorrow evening. We should know by then when you might arrive."

He persuaded her to drink the sweet tea that Kishen had quickly made and stood close to her until she had finished it.

"Come and lie down. You've had a shock. You were already tired. You need to rest."

He helped her out of her evening dress and, incredibly, as soon as she lay on the bed she fell asleep. Looking down at her, the immediate need to be strong and supportive over, he felt his legs might give way but gave himself a shake and, going back to the phone, rang Bob's number. Jess answered, her voice drowsy, but as soon as he told her what had happened she was instantly alert.

"Shall I come over?"

"No. It's alright. I managed to get Ann to lie down and somehow she's actually sleeping. What I really need is Bob's help to get her to England. I'll go to his office first thing in the morning and it would be good if you could come here then and stay with Ann while I'm out."

"Bob can drive over and collect you and drop me off. We'll be there at around eight. Give Ann my love when she wakes. Tell her that I'm coming. That I'm thinking of her. And Sam, look after yourself."

Throughout the night, Sam fell into a light doze from time to time but was instantly aware of Ann's slightest movement. She slept fitfully and restlessly, continually half waking to find him close beside her.

The next morning, her emotions tightly controlled, she followed her daily routine and was bathed, dressed and ready for breakfast by seven. Kishen and Sam both hovered over her but she seemed determined to carry on as usual. Kishen stood behind her chair, handing her toast or pouring tea the minute she finished either, such simple services his only way of expressing his feelings. Sam, falling in with her obvious need for normality, also tried to behave as always but he rang his secretary at her home to tell her what had happened and that he would not be in for work. He then called his parents, with whom he had a difficult conversation. He knew that all their instincts would push Zal and Perin into rushing straight over but, though he realised how hurt they would be, was adamant that Ann must be given time alone. In this he was unconditionally committed to her whatever the cost.

"She is in a very fragile state and simply can't deal with sympathy or other people's feelings. She'll leave for England as soon as possible. I'll let you know what's happening. I'll call later."

He was anxious about Ann undertaking this journey without him, regretting even more keenly the dark dissonance underlying their apparent harmony, but this was no time to raise the question of her continuing failure to make the necessary moves for their projected visit to her family and he simply said, "I hate the idea of your going through all this without me but the fact is that if I came with you it might make everything more difficult. I can't do anything to help. I'm still a stranger to your family and they shouldn't have to deal with the stress of that at such a time."

"I'm sorry, Sam. I'm so sorry. I've been stupid and selfish, but yes, I will have to go alone. It will be hard for you, left behind and left out. At least I know that you will be comfortable. Kishen will take good care of you."

They were taking longer than usual over breakfast, the weight of grief dragging them into slow motion and they were still at the table when Jess arrived. She went to kneel beside Ann.

"I won't say anything. Words can't help. Bob is going to arrange things so that you get home quickly and it might be best for us to keep busy and get you packed and ready. But we can talk if you need to. Whatever you want. Just tell me."

Bob followed her in and kissed Ann's cheek. "My dear girl. Count on us. I'll do all I can. I'm taking Sam off now and Jess will stay as long as you want her. I'll bring Sam back when we have sorted out a flight for you. I can't do much but I can deal with these lesser problems."

When he and Sam came back late in the afternoon, having dealt with all the necessary formalities and managed to get Ann on a flight very early the next morning, she and Jess had been busy enough to ensure that she was ready to travel but they had talked in a way that had left her exhausted. Seeing this, Bob, giving Jess a firm look, said that they would leave her to get some rest. As Sam went to the door with them, Jess spoke to him in an undertone.

"Sam, I don't want to be unkind but try to stop your parents coming to the airport. Your mother would be sensible but your father always wants to take charge of everything. Even he can't organise death and sadness. Best not to let him try." She reached up and hugged him. "Dearest Sam. Sorry. I shouldn't upset you. You could be forgotten in all this. Take care of yourself and call on me at any time if you need anything."

Ann's departure the next morning was as smooth as Bob could make it. Tall and commanding, he carved a way for her through the urgent motion of the crowded airport. She clasped his hand and thanked him and was then held closely by Jess for several moments.

"I'll be thinking of you every single moment. I'll be here for you as soon as you get back. Oh Ann, if only I could do something."

Jess was openly in tears and Ann gave her a further hug before firmly detaching herself. She and Sam had said their goodbyes at home and only embraced very briefly before she moved through the gate to the plane. It was a long walk. So much effort had gone into maintaining the wafer thin veneer of calm over her inner stress that her legs were weak and boneless. She found her seat in something of a daze and was hardly aware of the chattering passengers around her and, after take-off, even the steady hum of the engines could not deaden the ache of her thoughts as her mind trod and re-trod the paths that had led her to this bitter moment. The weakness of her legs spread through the rest of her body as she thought of how this journey would end. Once, she had not been afraid of the positive action that had started her on another difficult journey, but she saw now that her youthful self-confidence had been underpinned by a sense that everything she was ruthlessly rejecting would stand still, remain unchanged, be there if it should ever be needed again, and even the coldness between her father and herself hadn't destroyed this belief. That past and that confidence were now lost forever. It was true that in the days ahead of her she would have the company of people who had known her for most of her life, many of whom had also known Clifford for most of his, but her new existence was a blank to them, the country she lived in merely a geographic fact and her husband an unknowable entity. Then, in India, there would be no continuity to soften her loss, for Clifford's life had been nebulous to Zal and Perin, irrelevant to their own concerns and his death would not touch them. Sam only felt it because he loved her. Even for him it was a second-hand experience. A desolate perception, that finally every individual is unique and only protected from the loneliness of that uniqueness by living in a group and playing by the group rules, pinched her heart.

It was a long flight and, unable to free herself from these bleak reflections, she felt that it would never end but at last it was over. She was met by a cousin, her father's elder nephew, Charles, who greeted her kindly but calmly and, without any fuss or fanfare, her luggage was collected, the car located and they set out on the road to Norfolk.

"Father wanted to come and get you but I suggested that it would be best if I came. I thought it would be easier for you. You know how our elders always are. Frankly, I often don't know what is going on inside them." Her cousin looked sideways at her. "It is exactly how things were when you got married. I'm really sorry, Ann, that none of us came to your wedding. All the younger members of the family feel bad about it but we simply didn't know how to deal with them then either."

"Don't worry about that now. It's over. We have to concentrate on Mother's needs. How is she? Where is she?"

"At the farm, with your grandpa and grandma Fincham. That's where we're going, where you'll be staying. At least, until after the funeral."

This brutal word hammered reality into Ann's heart, reality that Edna's pallor and dark-ringed eyes rendered clearer and colder and, though her mother made a determined effort at self-possession, it was a shock to see that grief had physically diminished her. Always a small, trim woman, she now looked quite tiny.

Death had similarly diminished Clifford. Under a compelling urge, as if needing proof that they would never actually meet again, Ann was taken to the funeral parlour to see him. The large, vigorous man of her memories had gone and she stood for a long time, gazing down at this unnervingly small body which seemed impossibly frail to have contained the strong, potent force that had been her father. Having expected to be overcome by emotion, she found that these expectations themselves generated a degree of shaming theatricality in her that insulated her from the cruellest of her feelings, but she was shattered by a sense of awful finality. These were the worst moments of her farewell to her father, and the loneliest.

At the funeral, the shared familiarities of the service tempered sorrow and, as they all processed out of the small church and moved between the headstones, many of which bore the names of Bakers and Finchams, the gentle autumn sunlight and birdsong offered a more primitive consolation. Ann felt the soft warmth easing her taut shoulders and her hands unclenched but when, after the final rites, they walked away from the open grave, so neatly prepared with its discreetly covered mound of excavated earth to one side, the thought of that waiting darkness and cold, impossible to conceal, shuddered through her and her throat thickened with unshed tears.

Clifford, for all his inner secrets, had possessed a gift for friendship and everyone present truly mourned him yet, on their return to the farmhouse, the gathering very quickly took on a more social aspect and with the circling of food and drink there was almost a party atmosphere. Something had ended but the mourners closed ranks and made small talk again. Each of them had a private moment with Edna but they dispersed in a restrained public bustle. The family, spent and weary, went to bed to recover and prepare themselves for the continuation of their lives.

The next day Edna said she must go back to the cottage and get things in order there. Ann, in a rare gesture, held her mother's hand.

"Why don't we both do what's necessary and then arrange for you to come back and stay with me in Bombay for a month or so? I know that you will never get over this but that would give you time to come to terms with things in a new place. Somewhere without memories to continually trouble you. Do come, Mother. It would be good for me too."

In recent days Edna had been conscious only of a deep, draining exhaustion but Ann's suggestion roused her from this. "I'd feel like a deserter. It's as if my being here means that I'm still standing by your father. I don't want to upset you, but you know that he didn't want you to go to India and if I came it would seem like disloyalty."

This frank expression of what had always been left unsaid was not easy to deal with but Ann put her feelings aside and with some difficulty managed to persuade her mother to accept her invitation. Edna realised that her feelings were ambiguous. Clifford had been deeply wounded by what Ann had done and there was little doubt that his disappointment had affected his health, but it would be unfair to see this as the cause of his fatal heart attack and too harsh to blame her for his death. She regretted any mild antagonism that she couldn't repress and agreed to go to India, in part as a compensation for this; in part because, bereft of both her husband and her daughter, she dreaded the emptiness of her cottage; in part to escape from any possible negative views of this whole situation that might surface among her wider family. Her going would be an endorsement of Ann, a declaration of faith that would not only protect her daughter but also herself when she eventually returned. She knew that her parents would be somewhat scared by her venture. She hadn't allowed them to see how much she had longed to escape at the time of Ann's wedding and had soon apparently settled back into her habitual daily round after that fuss had died down. Now she was being unusually adventurous.

Clifford's father, however, approved her plan and said as much to Ann. "That's a good thing you are taking your mother back with you. She has missed you all this time. It's not the way we'd have liked things put right but it will make the best of a bad job."

He had been a widower for ten years, sharing and working his farm with his elder son James and his two grandsons, Charles and Peter. Perhaps living with a younger generation had widened his horizons. Whatever his thoughts about his granddaughter's marriage, he had seen Clifford's reaction to it as extreme, sensing something exaggerated in his nominally staid son that had offended his sense of propriety. During her visit he was calm and unemotional with Ann but this was his usual manner and he was the only one of her older relatives to touch on past difficulties.

Her decision made, Edna wanted to get away as soon as possible and dealing with immediate practical matters helped her to surmount any misgivings. There was time to sort out the cottage, arrange for its care and make sure that the woman from the village who had helped her for years would continue to come in to clean it regularly. There was also time to pick out clothes suitable for the Indian climate and buy any necessary extras but no time to worry or brood. Ann phoned Sam to prepare him for their arrival and Edna was greatly pleased to get a note from him.

24/9/68.

Dear Edna,

Forgive me for being so informal. Ann must have told you that she calls my mother Perin and I am fitting in with that. I want first to say how grieved I am for your

114

shocking loss. It is good that you feel able to come to us at such a time and that we shall have a chance to get to know each other better. I never had that opportunity with Ann's father. I met him so briefly and I now feel the sadness of that. I look forward to having you here and hope that you have a comfortable flight. I will meet you at the airport.

With affection and my warmest thoughts,

Sam.

The day before they left, the whole family, young and old, came together at the Finchams' for lunch. Though the usual hearty meal was served, this was a subdued affair, but all of them, whatever their private thoughts, felt the need to bid Ann a proper goodbye this time and to wish Edna well for her momentous journey. Charles had again volunteered to be the driver and came the next day to collect them. With typical country caution, they started out in very good time and had longer than necessary at the airport before their flight was called but soon enough Edna found herself, for the first time in her life, on an aircraft and, unbelievably, on her way to Bombay. She had dreaded this flight but only felt actual fear as they pulled away from solid ground. After that, there was no sense of motion as none of the usual markers of passing from here to there were available. The roar of the engines dulled to a monotonous drone and, after an initial bustle – seats adjusted, items taken down from overhead lockers, stewards summoned – all the passengers settled into torpor. Her own recent burst of activity over, Edna, overwhelmed by her previous tiredness, succumbed to the auditory hypnosis and spent much of the time asleep.

Ann looked at her mother's temporarily uninhabited face. The small death of people in sleep is always disconcerting but perhaps her mother had never been wholly present for her even when awake. Though overcome with grief at her father's death, she saw how temperate and measured her relationship with her parents had actually been. Allowing for the fluidity of definitions of love, she was sure that they had loved her, but within the limits imposed by an inherent mistrust of love's wilder possibilities. It was probably this long suppression of every visceral and primitive element of her nature that had caused the explosive effects of her meeting with Sam. All her new friendships had also proved to be a lesson in openness and warmth that had changed her considerably and she felt an unusual tenderness towards her mother, a strong sense of her vulnerabilities. She was overcome by an urge to protect her and, though she woke Edna for their two stopovers, was glad to see her taking this chance for a complete rest. She resolutely refused to examine the thought that this also saved them from an unaccustomed intimacy but did realise that this concentration on her mother was a distraction from her own unhappiness.

They landed in the early hours of the next day and it was two thirty in the morning when they emerged from customs. This was fortunate timing as Sam had no difficulty in coming to meet them alone at that hour. Edna's arrival in India was, consequently, less flamboyant than Ann's had once been. Though Bombay never ceased to pulse with life, it was at its most subdued and darkness hid the unlovely backdrop to their drive through the suburbs so her first impression of her daughter's urban surroundings was somewhat hazy. Then, after a bath and light snack, she was installed in the comfort of a well-appointed guest room, with time to recover from her travels and space to draw breath and prepare for whatever lay ahead of her.

ELEVEN

Ann decided that for Edna's first day, even though she could not be fully protected inside, she should not be exposed to the din and dazzle and all the inevitable shocks awaiting her outside. Bombay vibrated with its customary frenzied activity. Though unable to reach the back of their building, a succession of hawkers in a nearby side road created a continual, harsh cacophony. Among this endless crowd were sweet sellers and peanut vendors with their monotonous calls; fortune tellers parading a decorated cow and blowing conch shells; a scissor-grinder spinning his creaking wheel; a toy seller playing a rasping, single-stringed toy violin and pulling a rattling, articulated wooden animal behind her; men directing performing monkeys by banging out rhythms on small drums; street musicians and singing beggars; a key cutter jangling a bunch of keys and banging on an old bucket; men who traded in old newspapers and bottles with their drawn-out, haunting cries of 'Pa..a..a..per Walla..ah!' and the shrill and equally prolonged 'Tak..ee..ee...yeh' of the women who could be hired to chip away at, and make rough again, household grinding stones, smooth with use. These penetrating sounds rose above a background hubbub; crows cawed, dogs barked, children shrieked, broadcast film songs shrilled monotonously and endlessly from tinny radios, servants in nearby buildings pounded spices or thumped washing on bathroom floors, conversations like mini riots erupted and died down, traffic roared and hooted and gangs of masons banged and clanged as they worked on new buildings that would increase and re-echo these dreadful decibels. It was impossible to totally insulate oneself from this but Ann's flat was at a slight remove from it all and, in decorating it, peace and calm had been her theme. She intended to make full use of this to cushion her mother's introduction to the starker aspects of India. Any raucous sounds coming through in these first hours would at least be softened by pleasing surroundings.

Sam had taken the day off in order to be on hand if needed but he had breakfasted early and gone into the study to leave Ann alone with her mother. She had wondered if Edna would find the presence of the servants disconcerting, forgetting that her grandparents had always employed daily domestic help and that the men who worked on the farm treated the whole family with a laid-back respect. If there was a very East Anglian openness in these relationships, hers with Kishen was equally relaxed and friendly. Edna was quite at ease.

After a leisurely breakfast, they spent some time unpacking and then went out onto the balcony to enjoy the view of the sea. This was one of Ann's consolations, the visual balm of that gently moving blue expanse helping to neutralise the aural assault they were constantly under. She was expecting the Mehtas later. Perin was coming at eleven for coffee, while Zal would join them all for lunch. Knowing that she had hurt her in-laws by leaving for home without seeing them, she was anxious to set things right immediately. When Perin arrived, she was indeed noticeably cool but, within seconds, her genuine concern overcame any ruffled feelings.

"My dear girl, what terrible things we have to bear in this life. Remember that we too are your family and are here to help you." She turned to greet Edna. "It is good to be meeting you at last but sad that it has to be in such a way. We are all very much shocked by what has happened. I hope that these weeks with Ann will be a comfort for you. We understand that at first you will want to have a quiet time with her but we would like to share in making your visit as pleasant as possible when you feel able to go about more."

Edna had determined not to dwell on her grief but over their coffee somehow found herself talking very freely to Perin, and Ann, murmuring about lunch arrangements, left them alone together until Zal burst in on their gentle colloquy with florid sympathy. Over lunch he outlined elaborate ideas for Edna's entertainment. Prepared to be offended when Sam said firmly that they would take things slowly before starting out on anything resembling a holiday, he was appeased by Perin who told him that she and Edna, agreeing that this arrangement would give Ann time to re-enter her daily life and pick up any necessary domestic and social threads, had already planned to spend the following day together at Dahanipur House. He decided that his driver should collect Edna at ten the next morning and that Sam should bring her back on his way home from work.

Meanwhile, Ann had already invited Jess and Bob over for dinner that evening, keen for her mother to meet her closest friends as soon as possible. Edna immediately took to Bob. He was so like the men she was used to, reassuring, down-to-earth, large but undemanding and if Jess was somewhat more effusive than she usually found tolerable, she was charmed by her warmth and obvious affection for Ann.

The day at Dahanipur House, though it began badly, was equally satisfactory. Despite travelling in Zal's large, comfortable car, Edna was alarmed and overwhelmed by her first experience of Bombay by daylight. In her fifteen minute drive she saw more traffic and underwent more shocks and scares than in a lifetime of driving around Norfolk but, led by Perin into a wide, sunny balcony and served a tall glass of homemade lemonade, she quickly recovered and the two women, who had long been holding in an unexpressed sadness, soon found themselves deep in a far more revealing conversation than either had been prepared for; a conversation that eventually did much to restore them both.

They began by looking at photographs of the November reception at the Taj Mahal Hotel but Perin, sensing a distinct coolness in Edna's response to them, soon set down the leather album. "It is too sad that however hard we try, we cannot behave as we'd expected we would when our children married. I'd always looked forward to our elder son's wedding as an occasion that would be celebrated traditionally. There were so many things I had dreamed about and I put too many of those lost hopes into this party. I didn't mean to upset you with the pictures."

Edna replied with an equal frankness. "The wedding we had in England was not what I had dreamed of either. It was, in fact, sadly mean and makeshift and no one who mattered to me was there. I may not belong to a special community in the way that you do, but Clifford and I had always been very close to our families and friends and Ann's marriage made me ill-at-ease with them for the first time in my life."

"Naturally I can see what a shock Ann must have given you when she told you about Sam. We must not be unpleasant to each other but I can also see that you thought she was the one making the real mistake. Of course it was very hard for you. She was going far from home and changing her life completely but we did not feel less upset about Sam. Certainly we did not believe he was doing the best he could. There were girls we knew, of good Parsi families, who seemed to us far more suitable for him."

"It's too late to reproach each other over such things, Perin, or argue over the rights and wrongs of what happened. Our children are married. We have led very different lives but we are now somehow related. We have both been disappointed. I'm sure that we understand one another's feelings in a way that few other people can."

"I'm sorry. You are very right. I'm sure that, aside from all your natural fears, you felt the same pain that we did. Our children decided something so serious without our slightest knowledge that this was happening. All our hopes for them dismissed as unimportant."

"I don't think that they have the least idea of how hurtful it was to feel years of caring for them ignored. My husband, who was so close to Ann and had so many plans for her, never got over it."

Edna, who was not given to weeping, had difficulty in holding back tears and Perin patted her hand. "How you must grieve for him. He has lost so much that he still had to look forward to and for him to have also lost any chance of overcoming that disappointment is a terrible thing. I feel so deeply for you."

Edna's voice was steady but her cheeks were wet. "The one thing I must not do, is blame Ann for her father's death. I have been tempted to, but I know that he was at fault in expecting too much of her. He and I were very contented together all these years but he was clever in the way that people who love books are clever and I was never much of a reader. Ann is very like him and they enjoyed the same things. He planned for her to work with him. He never thought of her wanting a different life."

Perin again patted her hand. "I too have a clever husband and he too is not always sensible. You know, we fret so much about our children's marriage: it is unconventional, it will not work. But see! I married someone from my own community approved, no chosen, by my parents and yet I married a stranger. I met Zal very few times before our wedding. I will say something to you now that I have never said before to anyone. We are not at all close. We share less in our daily lives than Sam and Ann do. We knew the kind of life we would lead – our customs guided us there – but I have never talked to Zal as I am talking to you. I have been as lonely as Ann may sometimes be, so far from everything she is used to. But when she is lonely, Edna, she can talk to Sam. What a blessing for her. God is great."

"Oh Perin! In our generation and long before that, countless women must have known the kind of loneliness you're describing. I can't say that I have. Clifford was always my friend. But we only shared a part of his life." Edna's voice wavered. "He may have been the lonely one. Quite a large part of my time passed in a way that was somehow separate from being married. I can't describe things well but perhaps you see what I mean. In many ways I just went on as always.

My family were still at hand, I was living in the same place among familiar people and nothing changed drastically for me." She paused and looked down. "When we were young life was harder. So were we maybe. We did expect less and accept less. It isn't the obvious things about this marriage that frighten me. It's the fact that Ann and Sam have given up so much and put so much of themselves into it. When people have such faith in each other and their expectations are so high, there are dangers there. Little differences that we thought normal will always seem more threatening to them. And they are bound to happen. They always do happen, so easily … over such small things. We didn't want this marriage but we both want it to work. We just have to stand by and trust that all goes well."

They sat silent for a few moments and then Edna picked up the album that Perin had put down on the coffee table. "Do show me the rest of these photos. Ann sent me several but you have a lot more and besides you can tell me something about the other people in them."

The rest of the morning was spent agreeably and harmoniously and Zal's arrival for lunch struck something of a discordant note as he returned rather vehemently to his plans for Edna's stay.

"Sam is certainly overcautious. I understand that you are in mourning and would prefer not to be too sociable but we can take you about to see things that you must see while you are here. We would feel bad not to do as much for you as we can."

Although uncomfortable about this possible dissension between father and son, Edna had gained a lot from her day with the Mehtas and Ann and Sam were delighted by its obvious success. For Ann it seemed that a partial reassembling of her fragmented life had begun, while Sam had the sense of something healing having taken place and the guilt from which he could never totally free himself was somewhat eased. Edna then put an end to the rising tension between him and his father by persuading him to agree to many of Zal's plans. She convinced him that she was less unwilling to be active than he supposed, that going out would be good for her. So they embarked on a more adventurous programme than planned.

It began with a day spent in museums and places of worship. After trailing politely in Zal's wake around numerous temples and churches, Edna was glad of the quiet evening that followed. They began with a gentle stroll round the famous terraced gardens above the city, taking time to watch the sun set over the sea before moving on to mingle for a while with the regular crowd at the Gateway of India. From there they crossed to the nearby Taj Mahal Hotel, where, after a lavish dinner, she was shown the venue of the event she had seen in so many photographs.

Then, for two hectic weeks she seemed to spend a great deal of time in caves. Their names rang in her head – Kanheri, Elephanta, Ajunta, Ellora- but she ended up totally confused about which was which. When Zal began pressing for her to visit Delhi and Agra, suggesting that they should fly north for a few days, both Edna and Sam firmly rejected this idea as too ambitious. Sam, feeling that so far he had largely missed out on his chance to get to know his mother-in-law better, insisted that she should spend a quieter time at home before her return to England and as Ann, eager that they should be friends, was careful to leave them alone together on a variety of pretexts, he at last managed some serious conversations with her.

"I am haunted by the thought of you on your own when you get back to England, Edna." He looked anxiously at her. "By bringing Ann out here, I have made your present sadness and loss much worse for you and there seems little I can now do. You've been friendly and kind all this time but you must be angry with us both."

"I was never angry, Sam. Upset, of course, and worried about Clifford. I'll be honest with you about him. He was broken by what happened. Yet for years he'd been in the habit of suppressing his deepest feelings and our lives, apparently, just went on. We were so settled, so rooted in our ways that we didn't really have to try. What we'd always found unthinkable was change. Ann could have been like us. We thought she was. I can't blame her for being braver than we were and, though we both considered her foolhardy, I do see how well she is coping with any problems she faces. Don't worry about what you have done to my life, Sam, think about having made hers much harder and never let anything stop you from supporting her."

"That sounds as if you are indeed angry with me."

"No, I'm not. I have come to really like you and admire the way you are coping too. I can see the pressures you are under. Your family make continual claims on you and obviously you have to put a lot of effort into your job and concentrate on your future and your career. You have all that to deal with but you still give a lot of time to Ann and try to see things from her point of view. You are very good to her but I know how easily quarrels can erupt even between people who care deeply for one another and how small things can blow up into major misunderstandings. Try to stay cool whatever happens between you and remember that you have taken the place of Ann's family. All this rushing about has kept her from brooding over her father but she is extremely upset. "

"Don't worry. I promised to be everything to Ann when I asked her to come here with me and I mean to keep that promise." Sam couldn't resist a small retaliation, "You must have seen, though, that she has a lot of friends whose company she really enjoys. More friends than she had at home I think."

"I know that she has gained a lot, Sam. Just don't forget what she has lost, that's all I'm asking."

Even with all this ongoing family activity, Edna spent a considerable time with Jess. Ann had cancelled all her tuitions for a month but had felt obliged to continue with two pupils who only had a short time left with her before leaving India and Jess volunteered to keep her mother company while these necessary sessions lasted. Edna, though she found her an entertaining companion, was closely observant, indeed critical, of this girl who had become so important to her daughter, somewhat anxiously aware of the extent to which she could influence Ann's well-being.

"Sometimes I feel that Jess doesn't fully appreciate Bob," she ventured, when she and Ann were lunching alone for once. "She rather takes him for granted don't you think? She can be quite a flirt. It must upset him sometimes."

"I don't believe it does, Mother. He knows that she'd never do anything to really hurt him. Her parents are clearly so besotted with her that they have fostered a belief in her that everyone, including Bob, is happy when she is happy, so she does much as she pleases and doesn't always see how that affects other people, but she depends on Bob and she knows how much he does for her. She won't do anything to put that at risk."

Edna said nothing more but she had been driven to speak by a growing suspicion that Jess harboured more than friendly feelings for Sam. She did not believe that he was conscious of this. He seemed to react to Jess much as she herself did, taken by her charm, frequently amused by her but clear-headed about her faults. Ann, though so fond of her friend, was obviously not blind to these either and, if not entirely reassured, Edna largely stopped worrying. It had been an unusual intervention on her part but, like Ann before her, she had become more extrovert. India with its vehement and insistent assaults on their senses had taken and shaken them both. Edna, though, had less incentive than Ann to change. Her longstanding stolidity held her intact throughout every distressing or novel experience and after six weeks she was more than ready to get back to the slow rhythm of Norfolk.

Ann felt a similar readiness to return to the routines and challenges of her own daily life. This visit had gone some way towards easing her insecurities. She was, though voluntarily, a displaced person. The unresolved, if largely unacknowledged, tug-of-war between conflicting loyalties that had led to her reluctance to return to England had been overridden by the terrible news about her father and throughout her time at home, this conflict had been overshadowed by her concern for her mother. She had, though, soon realised that even in the face of catastrophe and despite her mother's grief, the smooth tenor of life within her family was essentially unbroken. She had forgotten just how matter-of-fact these people could be. Their lives rotated steadily in tune with the cycle of the farming year and, though even the prosperous among them experienced its hardships and inevitable losses, they had learned to accommodate these, carrying on because it was necessary to do so, because animals had to be fed and fields ploughed or harvested whatever one's problems or heartaches. She realised that her view of India was skewed. Millions of rural people there must keep to similar staid pathways. Thrown into the immediacy of Bombay, it had been easy to forget that it was its character as a melting pot that made it so vibrant and volatile. In comparing her two lives, it was unfair to equate it with her own small town. Nevertheless, her relatives' sober characters and their unexciting lives suddenly made her Bombay existence, despite its difficulties, an alluring alternative. She had wanted to come back to it and by also coming, her mother had reinforced this new confidence and made her feel that she had not irretrievably cut herself in two. She might now be able to move between India and Norfolk in a way that she had for so long supposed almost impossible.

When arrangements were made for Edna's return, she did feel that her mother's solitary flight would be a frightening undertaking but, as usual, Bob solved their problem. He introduced them to an Englishwoman of similar age, flying back to London after visiting her family, who would be glad of Edna's company for the journey. At the airport, Zal and Perin were effusive and Sam was emotional but mother and daughter were calm and undemonstrative. As Edna walked off with her new acquaintance, she turned at the last moment to exchange a long look with Ann. This time together had been a strengthening and affirmative event in their lives.

TWELVE

After her mother left it took about a week for Ann and Sam to settle back into their earlier habits and then, for a while, life appeared to go on as before. Though they had continued to see a great deal of Jess and Bob all this time, treating them as family, Edna's situation, her age and interests had prevented them from seeing much of their other young friends. An evening was arranged for them all to get together again and Ann was immediately approached by Hari.

"We were all saddened to hear about your father and glad that you have had your mother with you. My father died when I was a teenager. I know what a huge gap that opens up in one's life. Your foundations are rocked by an earthquake and everything seems unsafe and at risk. I do feel for you."

"Thank you. I didn't know that you had lost your father, Hari. It must have been hard at such a young age. It is frightening. As you say it takes the ground from under your feet."

"I imagine that it is particularly difficult for you. You are so far away from home and must worry about your mother being alone, without you or your father."

"Well, I hope to go and see her again before too long." She felt it necessary to explain that the community she came from belied any Indian perceptions of the coldness and unfriendliness of life in England. "Luckily she has her own parents still and a large family nearby and they all support each other and help each other through hard times."

"She is living in a rural area, though, and is somewhat isolated." Hari was still concerned.

"You have to forget everything that the word "rural" means in India. England is a very small country and, even though my relatives rarely visit it, London is less than a hundred miles away from our home. Everything is much cosier really.... if you can imagine what that is like."

She was aware of the constant possibility of such misunderstandings but sharing a sense of loss led them to speak more openly than ever before and Hari told her about the longer term effects of his father's death on his own life.

"If he had survived there is no doubt that I would have been pressured into marrying before now. I am almost thirty, which is quite an advanced age to have survived as a bachelor. The thing is that I had my mother and three sisters to look after and they certainly had no interest in seeing me married. They needed me too much themselves."

When they reached home Sam was somewhat abrupt with her. "You spent a lot of time with Hari this evening. You shouldn't let him monopolise you. He can be quite overpowering."

"He was very understanding and helpful actually. Apparently he lost his father when he was quite young and it's good to talk to someone who knows exactly what it feels like."

"Are you saying that I don't understand and that you can't talk to me?"

Sam rarely made open comparisons between himself and others. Without being obviously aware of how attractive and eligible he was, he had inevitably absorbed a sense of this from those around him and Ann's willingness to give up so much to be with him, though it had caused him some uneasy moments, had also bolstered this underlying feeling. Yet such confidence could not override a more deeply buried impression. As a child he had frequently been praised but never caressed and kissed. Before meeting Anne he had always felt worthy but unlovable and whenever he worried about her, agonised over her reactions to India or felt the responsibility laid on him by her leaving so much behind, he was subconsciously driven by a dread of the loss of love. The memory of her coldness when she heard about her father had been working on him and he had not forgotten her words and her accusing tone, "Don't. What have we done? Don't touch me." He had convinced himself that this had been a momentary feeling induced by shock but since her return from England and throughout her mother's visit she had been less affectionate than usual. He had supposed that Edna's presence was somewhat inhibiting but even after her departure, Ann still seemed introspective and aloof.

"Are you missing your mother?" he asked her.

"I'm missing my father." Ann said sharply.

Sam winced. "You do think that I can't understand that. I just thought that having your mother here seemed to have helped and that it is harder for you now that she has gone."

"What is hard and was hard while she was here – on her own as I'd never seen her before, being part of our life in the way I'd hoped both my parents might – is thinking of all the years my father should have had and will never have. All the things he hasn't shared with us and will never share."

Sam put his arms round her. "I can't do anything except love you, Ann. It hurts me to see you like this, but that's all I can do, love you."

"Perhaps we've put too much faith in love, Sam." Ann's voice was edged with tears. "We thought it was everything, that we couldn't live without it. We simply didn't realise that there were many things that we could find it wrenching to live without."

Sam bent to rest his cheek on the top of her head. With a deep sigh, she put her arms round him and they leant against each other without speaking. These moments of physical closeness held them steady. Led by a sense of the pitfalls of speech for those whose language had evolved from such divergence, they always found solace in these more direct ways of communicating but, during the next six months, even these were apt to fail them.

In the weeks after her father's death Ann had concentrated first on her mother's grief and then on making Edna's stay in India successful. Now, she felt alone with her own sorrow and regret. At some level, her mind continually recycled images of death and impermanence that would suddenly surface in a vague but overwhelming dread. Often in their most intimate moments she would find herself paralysed by an appalled sadness and though Sam tried to stay sympathetic, he was young. Love for him could not be passive and patient. It surged through him and demanded a response. Increasingly meeting a barrier, a chilly apathy, it lost something of its energy and impetus. For the rest of that year they both tried to ignore all this. Ann battled to overcome her unexpected listlessness. Sam struggled to offer her loving support. Often he barely achieved tolerance. Only the necessity of meeting everyday demands enabled them to continue without any overt acknowledgement of their problems.

Since returning to Bombay, Ann, who had long shared most of her feelings with Jess, was finding being with her friend increasingly comforting. Her openness and honesty in facing up to and discussing what had happened was a huge relief after the constraint and discomfort felt by most people confronting bereavement.

"It makes me cry to think that your poor father wasn't given the chance to come here and see how good things are for you. He was worrying unnecessarily about you and that would have made him happy again. Oh Ann, you don't deserve this. Whatever you do, never think that you are to blame for all this sadness."

She burst into tears and Ann, who had shed very few, finally found herself also weeping freely. Jess hugged her.

"I have never felt so bad about anything in my life before but at least you have had your mother here. I do like her. She is so calm and sensible. Now promise that you won't worry about her, Ann. You must think of yourself now. Try to be happy. We all love you and we will always be here for you."

Even with Jess Ann had always drawn the line at talking over any difficulties between herself and Sam but she was sufficiently concerned about her current moods and the effects that they were having, to finally touch on this forbidden topic, though she was still unable to bring herself to admit just how bad she felt things to be.

"I am giving Sam a hard time. It's as if I were punishing him for what's happened to me. We must try to get Sam and Bob together as much as we can. Sam enjoys Bob's company and, more importantly, he can talk to him. More frankly than with anyone else he knows. He has never really had a serious male friend before. Being able to express his feelings as openly as he does with Bob does him so much good."

Jess was always ready to fall in with anything that meant being with Sam and Ann and though Bob was tied by an increasing work load, he enjoyed spending what free time he had with them rather than any other friends and their informal evenings and seaside weekends did become more frequent. Being with these trusted companions provided a space in which any tensions between her and Sam were put on hold and this gave Ann a sense that things were less changed than she sometimes feared.

She wrote home often. It was easier now that Edna had seen the places and people that she was writing about. It was no longer necessary to insert paragraphs of description and explanation at every point. She received robust and cheerful replies but her mother continually spoke of hoping to see her in England. Ann's feeling that a visit home was now possible persisted and she fully intended to take Sam but, somehow, the trip got delayed from month to month until, early in 1970, two things happened to make it recognisably impractical; Sam was promoted and as a consequence found his job once again extremely demanding, with any possibility of leave temporarily on hold and, shortly afterwards, Ann received the unexpected offer of a part-time teaching post at a nearby girls' college.

This was the result of the surprising possibilities of Bombay, where personal contact often replaced more formal procedures. Somehow, the Catholic nuns who ran the college had heard about her tuitions and wanted her to give their senior pupils twice-weekly classes in written and spoken

English. She was gratified by this chance to work on a more serious level but, worried about her lack of professional experience, felt the necessity for a great deal of study and careful preparation and had to spend considerable time in marking the various assignments that she set her new pupils. Her time was fully taken up by all this and there was no chance of a holiday in the immediate future. She was moving in a direction that she had never contemplated and it was an exacting, if exciting, progression. She found herself turning to Sam for advice and encouragement and this brought out an undervalued aspect of their ties to each other, rebuilding a bridge between them, a cooler, less electric connection, which, in itself, made them aware of how much they had changed. They were pierced by a poignant regret. Neither they nor anyone close to them had ever imagined how conventional their life would so quickly become, with its concentration on the mundane deadening its passionate and emotional heart. They had believed themselves special, seen themselves as embarking on something new and undiscovered. They had secretly seen themselves as pioneers, rejecting the humdrum, commonplace lives of their parents and it was disconcerting to have reached this well documented juncture.

By the end of that year they were getting to grips with their new responsibilities and as the external pressures eased, their inner sense of loss intensified, causing renewed tensions that made them increasingly touchy and irritable with each other. Perin, usually so discreet and undemanding, eventually found it impossible to stay quiet.

"Ann, I have never interfered between you and Sam. You have always realised that I was unhappy when he married you but I think that you know how much I, both Zal and I, have come to appreciate you. We have seen you make a very comfortable home for Sam and he has been able to get on in his company because of that. It may seem an old-fashioned attitude to you but seeing him properly cared for and doing well was very important to us. Perhaps you think that I saw looking after Sam and having his children as your duty. I do hope for grandchildren but I knew from the first that, after a time, you would need something to replace the work that you had always expected to do. I was very pleased when you started to teach and did well at that. Then you were taken up by the college. God is great. What you can't know is that I have often envied you, envied the way that you shared everything with Sam. What has happened? I understand how distressed you were about your father and what a shock it was for you. I think you believe that because we never knew him we can't share your feelings. Of course we can't grieve as you do but we can grieve for you. I know that we never get over these things but we have to accept sorrow in our lives. It is now so long since your father died and this still seems impossible for you. Whatever hurts you, hurts Sam and he is very unhappy these days. I know how your father felt. I have talked with your mother. I don't want to be hard on you but remember that when you married you made a choice. You chose Sam. You can't now change that and choose your father. I feel for you but I don't like to see my son upset. What is to be done?"

Ann had supposed that the studied respect that they had first shown each other had long since turned into something much warmer and her mother-in-law's clear-sighted analysis of her behaviour stung her.

"You think that I have broken the promise I made you when we first spoke to each other – the promise to do my

137

best. I have tried, Perin. At the moment, I just don't have the same energy that I started out with"

"Think of what has happened to you. You came out to us on a great wave of emotion. You were sad to leave your home and family. You may secretly have been afraid. You were certainly excited. It was a bold step. Any young girl would have been fired up. Sam – and I am praising my own son – was himself thrilling to you. If it was difficult for you here in the first years, something new, something interesting was always coming up. Then too, you were carried along by the feeling of how well you were doing. How could this go on, Ann? We aren't film heroines. Life can't always be a drama. You are suddenly looking at your life with Sam differently because of a terrible tragedy, but everyone eventually has to settle for a quieter happiness. Indeed that, or worse, less than that, is what some people have to content themselves with from the start. Don't forget what you have or how lucky you are to have it."

Ann was stunned into silence. Perin gently patted her cheek.

"I don't say all this angrily or idly. Something has to be done. I have been thinking how it would be for you to spend a little time away from Sam. Do you realise that you have never been apart except when you had to go to England and that was not an auspicious time? If you now went there together it might cause other problems for you. I have a suggestion. You will be having a Christmas vacation soon and what I plan would not interfere with your college work. You and Sam have hardly moved away from Bombay. You've spent all your holidays as we spend them, in the usual places in this area. It really is time that you saw more of the country. Do you remember my cousin, Freni Panday? You met her the day that you arrived in Bombay."

"Yes I do. I thought she seemed interesting but we hardly spoke to each other. I didn't know her other name was Panday. Didn't she say that she lived in Delhi?"

"Yes. Her husband, Rustam, is a successful businessman and they have a lovely home there, know everyone important in the city and go to all the smart functions. I've spoken to them and they would love to have you for a visit. They have no children and enjoy having young guests. Freni's father was a surgeon. She is highly educated and would be good company for you. It would be an interesting trip and would help you and Sam to step aside from each other for a while and give you a chance to think things over."

When this was put to Sam, he became quite angry.

"What on earth is my mother interfering for? And you Ann! You have never listened to your own mother. Why are you so ready to fall in with anything that my mother suggests?"

"Sam! Don't be so unfair. You have always been delighted whenever your mother and I have arranged anything together. At least when it was for your benefit! Admit that things between us have become strained lately. Possibly we have begun to take each other for granted and a short separation may help. I'll have a chance to see Delhi and we'll have something new to talk about when I get back."

"I don't take you for granted at all. On the contrary, I've been worried sick about losing you. So often lately you seem to have been rejecting me. I can't bear it and here you are talking like a tourist, promising me a travelogue and a few souvenirs."

"Oh Sam," Ann's voice was sad, "we've never been petty minded with each other before. Be reasonable. I'm only going away for three weeks. I'm not leaving you. It may do us some good. It can't do us any harm."

THIRTEEN

Once Ann had left for Delhi, with his reluctant assent, Sam returned to the flat every evening to find himself caught up in recollections of his earlier life without her. Her departure was a sharp reminder of the self-contained bleakness that she had rescued him from and, because he was accustomed to the companionship and closeness that their recent troubles had interrupted and diminished but not destroyed, his renewed loneliness had a crueller edge to it. They had pleased one another in so many ways, not least in their moments of light-heartedness and their shared private jokes, a frivolous froth on their deeper feelings that was particularly symbolic of his escape from the austerity of his childhood. What had happened to them? He reproached himself for his carelessness. He had denied taking Ann for granted but what respite had he ever given her. They had been so determined to create a good life together and prove those who doubted them wrong that he had lost sight of what was important. Overly influenced by his father's insistence on material success and intent on showing himself able to care for Ann, he had allowed such things to dominate their life. He hadn't taken holidays seriously, merely following in his parents' footsteps and seeing them as a necessary break from his job. Ann had made such an effort to adjust to her new life, had dealt with everything it threw at her, only to suffer a crushing personal loss. Why was he grudging her a real holiday? Why had he been so unutterably stupid? Why hadn't he shown her more of India? Why hadn't he taken her to Delhi? How had he allowed things to get to a stage when she was there without him – when she wanted to be there without him?

He felt no desire to see other people. Even the thought of being with Jess and Bob made him feel worse. He wanted no reminders of a happier state. He stayed in his office till late, trying to tire himself out by working and spent his short evenings and sleepless nights in a daze of unhappiness. A week later a letter arrived that did little to settle him.

28/12/70

Dear Sam,

Are you getting on alright alone? I'm sure that you are. Kishen is in virtual command of all our domestic affairs these days and will be looking after you beautifully. I'm having such a good time! The thought of staying so long with strangers did make me uneasy but I can't tell you how comfortable I am with Freni. She and Rustam have made me so at home. She's a great reader like me and not only has she read widely in English, she also reads French literature – in French!!! She is introducing me to French writers in translation! She says that her father, like mine, was a bibliophile and had a huge library. It seems impossible that we've had time for books. We go to a lot of parties. On Christmas Eve we went to a grand affair at the British High Commission. I met several people who know Bob. They all like him as much as we do. I've already seen a lot of Delhi. I'll spare you a travelogue!!! I have got you some souvenirs though!! We went to a fascinating market which houses Tibetan refugees selling their products. I couldn't resist some copper ornaments that we certainly don't need and I bought you some interesting prints that I think you will love. The weather is making everything so pleasant. Your mother told me that it could be quite cold and sent me here with all the necessary cover-ups, but I still can't believe that I'm wearing a thick coat and stockings in India! Yet, though it's cold, it's sunny and bright. It's perfect! Do you know, we even have porridge for breakfast sometimes! That's what my grandmother calls a frost-fighting start to the day. Freni's father went to Edinburgh University and she says that he returned with a degree in medicine, a weird taste for porridge that became part of the family menu and a tendency to call her lassie that made her feel like a sheepdog!!! She is enormous fun, Sam. She reminds me of Jess. She's so frank but never offensive. She was shocked that I'd been in India for five years and had never seen the capital. I told her that I have elderly relatives in Norfolk who have lived in a much smaller country for over fifty years and never seen its capital. She said that it was amazing that someone so enterprising should have come from such a stick in the mud bunch. I won't burble on. I wanted you to know how much I'm enjoying myself. And!! I still have another two weeks! Take care of yourself till I come back.

Much love,

Ann.

He read and re-read this. Just holding it seemed to connect him to her but he was left irritable and edgy. He knew that he should be delighted that she was getting on well with his relations and that she was happy but he could not supress a shamefaced resentment. There was no sign of the continually serious and sometimes sombre Ann of recent months nor, in this plethora of exclamation marks, of the pedantic English student she could be. High spirits burst off the page like champagne bubbles. She was not missing him in the least. He got himself a drink and sat for at least an hour in a miasma of mingled anger and desolation. Slowly he began to cool down and regain control over this unaccustomed and unwelcome agitation. He was able to see how it was that Ann, distanced from all that had been troubling them, the focus of the loving attention of so compatible a companion as Freni, had been swept up into this carefree mood, allowing herself to be impulsive and gay, not to hurt him, but to heal herself. He remembered his self-reproaches and roused himself to plan positively for her return. He would arrange for a trip to South India as soon as it was feasible so that they could explore another side of the country together. He began to make enquiries about locations like Kerala or Hyderabad. Their work schedules would mean it was impossible to go immediately but at least he could present Ann with a fixed plan and give her something to look forward to.

Then this mood of optimism was completely shattered. At work, he was asked to contact Hari to check on a bill that had been presented for recent supplies. It was a matter that needed to be handled with tact and, as someone who knew Hari well, he was considered the best person to deal with it, but he was only able to speak to a secretary.

"I'm sorry. Mr Chand is out of Bombay at present. He is on a short business trip to Delhi. I have all the details that you need and can send them to you if you like. I'll get Mr Chand to call you when he returns."

Sam put down the phone and gazed at it wildly. Every memory of Ann and Hari chatting at various gatherings rushed in on him. He had been aware of a spark of interest between them but had never been seriously troubled by it. Now, re-living that challenging moment when Ann had told him how easy it was to talk to Hari about her father's death, he felt a growing fear that in opening himself up to happiness he had also exposed himself to possible misery. This was the danger that he had sensed since he was a child and in every other aspect of his adult life he had maintained his alert self-protectiveness. Only with Ann had he surrendered control.

He put his head in his hands and told himself that he was going crazy. Delhi was a big city. Ann and Hari could inhabit its spaces without ever meeting. Ann was constantly with Freni, who might be modern and go-ahead but was still in certain respects as conservative as the rest of her kind. However much she indulged her guest, she was entertaining her at the request of a cousin and would take her unacknowledged, but clearly understood, role of chaperone and quasi-guardian seriously. He groaned. He could hardly believe himself capable of such irrationality and melodrama. He had so recently repented of behaving badly towards Ann and been planning to make it up to her. How could he so quickly allow himself to think of her in such a way? He made a strenuous effort to dismiss these perverse thoughts, forcing himself to be sensible and stay calm. Then, a few days before she was expected back, he received a second letter from Ann.

Dearest Sam,

I know you expect me back on the 14th but this is to say that I want to put off my return for just a little longer. Freni wants to take me into the Himalayas!!! Can you believe that I'm writing that? It's like another fairy tale! We're off on a flying, four day visit to Mussoorie. She says that, though it is very much out of season, I really should see what a hill station is like while I am in such close proximity to one and learn just how cold India can really be! This has only been mooted because we have the chance to drive up with friends of hers who own a property there and have to deal with some problem relating to it. They will stay on longer but will send us back with their car and driver. The plan includes an overnight stopover at your old school on the way up. They all know a teacher we can stay with. I would definitely like to see a place that played such an important part in your life. You will be cross. Of course it would be ideal if we could do this together but when would that happen? I am being a little disingenuous here because there won't be time to alter these arrangements whatever you say. In fact we leave tomorrow morning. I thought of phoning you but I was afraid that we might argue and that is the last thing I want just now. I'll get Rustam to post this. By the time it reaches you, I will probably be back in Delhi and will soon be home. Be patient with me. It's only another week. I'll settle down again when I get back. I *feel so much better and more cheerful. I promise to be less difficult and things will be fine. I love you.*

Ann.

At this point Sam felt inert and deadened. He was unused to putting himself through emotional hoops in this way. It was Friday evening. At work he had been in contact with people in a way that had taken the edge off his troubled thoughts and held the continual ache inside him just below consciousness but he felt a continued revulsion at the thought of seeing anyone socially. He faced a lonely weekend. He sat down once more with a drink and a book, trying not to think at all. He heard the phone ring and Kishen came in to say that Jess Memsahib was on the line. He was beaming. Jess was a favourite. Sam, for all his reluctance, had to rouse himself and take the call.

"Sam, I've just heard from Ann that she isn't coming home for some days yet. You won't believe this, but Bob has also gone up to Delhi. There is some emergency at work that requires discussion at a higher level. I never know the details of these things but it must be really important for him to go off on a Friday and work over the weekend. He'll only be there for two days. It's unlikely that he will get to see Ann. She seems to have been away for ages. I've missed her so much. Are you lonely Sam? Bob has only just left and I am already *so* lonely. What I thought was that we could go out to Mahu. Spending time there would cheer us both up. Do let's."

"How can we? Be sensible, Jess. It would look odd for the two of us to be there without Ann and Bob."

"What nonsense. Anyway, who would know we were there? And we're such an antisocial lot when it's the four of us together that we don't know the people in the other bungalows nearby except to nod to and they probably have no idea who belongs to whom among us, so even if they are staying there now they won't be at all surprised. Besides, we are old friends and everyone is used to seeing us with each other. Do say yes, Sam. I can't bear the thought of the next few days without all of you. It's *so* dismal without Ann and Bob. I miss them both. I can't see that it's necessary not to be able to see you either. Please. Let's go."

Sam said nothing for a while. It wasn't a good idea. People loved a gossip and however long-standing their friendship, however innocent this proposed trip, most of them would consider it unsuitable for Jess and himself to stay alone together. Then he thought about Anne's letter. She hadn't even phoned him, hadn't wanted to speak to him. He could spend two miserable days brooding on her casual treatment of him. He took a breath. "Alright. We'll go. But a shorter stay than usual. I'll pick you up at ten tomorrow morning. We'll come back by the middle of Sunday afternoon."

"Oh Sam, you are my favourite person. See you tomorrow. I'll take all the food that we need. You don't have to bother about a thing."

As he put the phone down Sam shook his head. What difference did the length of their stay make? What a fool he was. He was furious with himself. He had plenty to bother him. It was sheer idiocy to add to his problems. However he was committed and soon enough, they would be able to tell Ann and Bob about their impromptu jaunt.

When he arrived to collect Jess, her cook and bearer came out with a large ice-box, a suitcase and several smaller packages. They greeted Sam cheerfully. He was so frequent a visitor that they considered him almost one of their household.

"I said that we are going on a picnic with friends and that we will be staying with them tonight."

Jess settled herself in the seat beside him and he glanced sideways at her, thinking that if she felt the need to give her servants false explanations she must have doubts about what they were doing. The thought plunged him into a rather grim silence but she ignored this and told him all about her week, Bob's unexpected call to Delhi and her recent letter from Ann.

"She seems to love Delhi so much that she's almost forgotten all about us. She's obviously very fond of Freni. I'm quite jealous. My nose is definitely out of joint. We must have a wonderful, welcome-home party for her to remind her that she belongs with us."

"Neither of us should begrudge her any enjoyment after all that she's been through. She needed this break and Freni has been perfect company for her." Sam's voice was level and firm.

"I know. I know. I'm being mean. Don't worry. I'll forgive her as soon as I have her here with me. By the way, did you know that Hari has also been in Delhi? Everyone seems to be there except us. I wonder if he met Ann."

Sam gave her a very forbidding look and Jess hastily began to talk brightly about all the social and cultural events they could all share as soon as they were reunited. Ignoring the mayhem around them, she continued to chatter inconsequentially for the rest of the drive though Sam, concentrating on avoiding the crowds of people and animals through which they were fighting, made only the most perfunctory responses.

It was reasonably cool at this time of the year and although it was already past midday when they arrived, they went down to the beach for a quick swim before lunch. As they splashed into the water, Jess caught Sam's hand.

"Don't be cross with me. I know how bad things have been for you lately and I didn't mean to hurt you by talking about Ann as I did. That's the last thing I want to do. We've come here to cheer ourselves up and be happy."

"Let's forget it." Sam pulled away from her and swam vigorously out into the bay as he always did. Jess remained in the shallows and when he returned he found that she had gone back to the house and was already preparing their food. They both seemed intent on keeping to their accustomed ways and after lunch, spent the afternoon in the garden. Jess kept the conversation light and impersonal and Sam gradually lowered his guard and became more talkative. They had the usual evening snack and went for a moonlight swim. As they re-entered the bungalow, Sam yawned. "I'm very tired Jess. I've had a terrible week. I'll say goodnight and see you in the morning."

Jess made a move towards him but he turned away, walked quickly into his room and firmly closed the door. Once in bed, however, he tossed and turned for nearly two hours. What had he been thinking of to come here? He wanted Ann. The emptiness of the space beside him was almost tangible. His longing was a physical pain. At just after midnight he gave up trying to sleep and went out into the garden. He sat there for a long time, soothed by the cool and quiet of the night. Everything around him, the waves whispering across the sand, the leaves sighing in the trees, conjured up the softness, the tenderness that he was yearning for. The moist night breeze moved across his bare chest like caressing hands. He slowly drifted off into the dreamy, sensual state that Mahu so often induced, his limbs heavy and his eyes beginning to close but after a time, feeling somewhat chilled, he stood up, stretched, yawned and went back into the house.

"What's the matter, Sam? Can't you sleep?" Jess was standing there looking slightly tousled and droopy eyed. Before he could answer she came over and, standing very close, looked up at him, her eyes wide and her mouth tremulous.

"Oh Sam, I hate to see you like this."

He gazed down at her vivid little face and with a sharp intake of breath bent and kissed her hard on the mouth. Then, as if burnt, he jerked his head up and tried to step back but she put her arms round his waist and slid up to bury her face in his neck. He stood rigid and, with his hands on her shoulders, tried to push her away but she clung on, her face still hidden. Neither of them had spoken a word. They were caught up in a strange, silent struggle and feeling the insistent pressure of her damp and still slightly salty body, Sam suddenly lost all control and holding her as close as it was possible for them to be, kissed her all over her face and shoulders. He could not stop this madness and somehow they were in her room and on her bed in a naked tangle of limbs and searching lips.

It was quickly over. Sam rolled off the bed and sat in a bedside chair. "Oh God! What have we done?"

This struck him as a dreadful reminder of Ann's hateful, remembered words and he put his head in his hands. Jess got up and came over to him. She put her hand on his arm but he knocked it off. "Don't. Just don't touch me." Again the powerful echo of Ann's voice seared him. "Don't come near me."

"Don't be so fierce, Sam. What we have done isn't so terrible. I care so much about you. You seemed *so* miserable, *so* alone. I just wanted to comfort you."

"Comfort! I'll never be comfortable again. Oh God! I'll never dare to go near Ann. How will I even look at her? How can I have done this to her?" He looked distractedly around him. "This is more than terrible. It's appalling in so many ways. You are her dearest friend. This is the one place where she was always completely happy and we've destroyed it for her. We'll never be able to come here together again." He leapt up. "I can't stay here. It's unthinkable. We must go. We have to go. Now."

"How can we? Don't be so unreasonable. I can't go back in the middle of the night. What will the servants think?"

"Say that you suddenly felt ill. You've acted the part of Ann's loyal friend. You've acted the part of Bob's sweet little wife. You can play the emergency patient. Get dressed. Pack your things. We're going."

Jess had never doubted that everyone who knew her either loved her or liked her. No-one had ever spoken to her harshly before and this was Sam, who had always treated her with a slightly amused but gentle indulgence and who had just swept her into a fever of feeling deeper than she had ever been capable of. She could hardly recognise him and his uncharacteristic ferocity both shocked and repelled her.

"Sam! How can you speak to me like that? How can you be so unjust? It isn't like you to be rude and unkind. I know that we shouldn't have done what we have and that you are very upset but however bad you feel, please don't treat me this way."

Blind to the unfairness of his rage, his unpleasant stridency, Sam was unable to control this frightening loss of his customary decency, all his latent Puritanism, fuelled by shame and self-disgust, boiling to the surface.

"I said get packed. We're going."

She put her hand out to him, then, seeing his thunderous face, turned away trembling and went into the bathroom. Sam heard the shower running and went into his own room, hurriedly pulling on his clothes without even washing. By the time Jess had dressed and come out with her suitcase, he had gathered all their other things together, piled them in the car and was standing beside it, desperate to go. She hesitated in the doorway and seemed about to say something but he stopped her with another fierce glare. She waited for him to fetch her case but he got into the car without speaking and she carried it down the path, put it onto the back seat herself and climbed in beside him. She had barely closed her door before he shot off, racketing along the track at a reckless speed.

"Slow down, Sam! You are driving like a madman." Jess sounded really scared.

He eased down for a few moments but as they came out onto the main road accelerated again and they roared through the empty suburbs. Jess cowered in her seat, her head down, afraid of provoking him to greater excess, but as they came to the outskirts of the city she gathered her strength, sat up straight and said firmly, "Sam, you have to calm down. Think of how this looks. You can't let anyone see you in this state. You are acting like a lunatic. We have to be sensible. We can't allow this to go any further. We'll have to behave as though it simply hasn't happened. If we can't find a way of being natural and normal when we see Bob and Ann we are going to turn a mistake into a catastrophe."

He turned to her his face distraught. "God! I'd forgotten Bob in all this. I'll never be able to meet him again. I can't believe I've been such a swine."

The car had slowed somewhat but he put his foot down hard again, shooting forward so suddenly that Jess, thrown violently backwards, had to hold onto the sides of her seat and, just at that moment, another car emerged from a dark side road to their left and screeched to a halt in front of them. Sam wrenched on the wheel and swerved violently to the right. He tried to come back to the centre of the road but could not get the car under control. It skidded across the tarmac with a grinding shriek and slammed into the compound wall of a roadside apartment building.

FOURTEEN

Ann and Freni got back to Delhi at midnight on Saturday. It had been an enjoyable trip but they had covered a considerable distance in just four days and were both very tired. The following morning, Ann slept until well after ten, only waking when Freni sent in a servant with a tray of tea and toast and she was not bathed and dressed until after eleven. As she went down the stairs she was very surprised to see Bob outside in the porch with Freni and hurried through the open front door with a wide smile and outstretched hand.

"Bob! It's lovely to see you but what on earth are you doing in Delhi?"

"An emergency work meeting." Bob did not return her smile and was unusually abrupt.

Ann gave him a puzzled look and Freni said gravely, "Bob needs to talk to you, my dear. Take him into the drawing room and I'll see that you are not disturbed."

Ann, startled and alarmed, led the way through the hall into a large room on the left. Bob closed the door behind them and then turned to face her, looking pale and upset.

"What is it, Bob? I'm getting scared. Tell me. You never shilly-shally. What is it?"

Bob came forward and took her hand. "Ann, something terrible has happened. I hardly know how to tell you but

I *do* have to tell you and there is simply no way to soften my news." He took a deep breath and reached for her other hand. "It's Sam. In the early hours of this morning, he had a car accident – a fatal accident. He died instantly."

Ann snatched her hands away and fell into a chair, her arms folded around her chest as if holding herself together. When at last she managed to speak, she sounded weirdly calm and detached. "I've been unkind to Sam since my father died. I thought that his death was terrible, the most terrible thing that had ever happened to me."

She sat quite still for a minute, a strange, reflective look on her face, before continuing in the same quiet tone, "I didn't know what terrible was. They are both dead and I'll never be able to tell either of them how sorry I am for the way I treated them."

Suddenly, she raised her head and pressed her hands flat against her stomach as if forcing out and drawing up pain from somewhere deep inside her. It seemed to move visibly through her stretched throat, to be expelled in a prolonged, silent scream. Bob had never seen such a raw, physical manifestation of anguish. He knelt down and put his arms round her without speaking. There was nothing to say. She slumped back limply against him, shaken by tearless sobs.

Freni came in and stood beside them, her face contorted. "My dear, dear girl. Oh my dear girl. What can I do for you? Can I get you anything? Something to drink? A brandy? Oh my dear girl."

She was unable to say anything more. Bob had described the accident to her and knowing how Jess was involved, she foresaw heartache for Ann beyond this harsh grief.

Bob held Ann more closely and said over his shoulder, "Perhaps it would be a good idea to get her a drink. Something hot might be best."

Freni nodded and went out and Ann slowly quietened. Bob sat back, holding on to her hand and, at last, she looked him full in the face. "Is Jess in Delhi with you? If only I could see Jess."

Bob's face crumpled and he again put his arms round her. "Ann, we have to talk about what has actually happened."

She bent forward and laid her head against his shoulder. "I'm sorry. I can't seem to be sensible. Awful waves of pain keep sweeping through me and all I can hear are those dreadful words – he died instantly." She broke into fresh sobs.

Bob held her for a few moments without speaking but then straightened her and said gently,

"I know. I know. But we must talk."

With a huge effort, she stopped crying. "I'm listening. Tell me what you have to tell me."

"You need to be brave, Ann. It's very bad. Jess isn't here in Delhi. She was in the car with Sam when the accident happened. She's in hospital in Bombay. I have to go back today. The thing is…….."

She interrupted him, "I don't understand. Why were Sam and Jess together? Where were they going? What were they doing, driving out at that hour?" She rubbed her hand across her forehead and said wearily, "No. I can't think about it. I can't deal with it. It's all too much."

Bob stood up as Freni re-entered the room. She handed Ann a cup and sat down beside her in his place. "Drink this, dear. It will help you."

Ann drank a little and then set the cup aside. She again sounded unnaturally calm.

"Freni, I'll have to speak to Zal and Perin."

"Don't worry about that. I've just had a call from Zal and I've spoken to both of them. They know that Bob has told you what has happened, that he is taking care of you and will travel back to Bombay with you."

Bob intervened, "I know how harsh this sounds but we have to discuss getting back, Ann. You need to come with me tonight." He hesitated and then added quietly, "You realise that Sam's family will be arranging a....will go ahead with a..." for the first time he faltered.

Ann was rigid and her tone controlled, "You mean a funeral."

Bob looked haggard, "I can hardly bear to think of it. I can only imagine your feelings. I can't find adequate words….." Again he came to a stop.

"We do have to find words, though, however appalling it seems." Freni had regained her composure and now put her hand on Ann's arm. "I have to say these things to you now, Ann. You have to know what you need to do. We don't have the luxury of time. Bob is right. Everything will happen very quickly. Usually our funerals take place immediately, but in the case of accidents some delay is possible. Still, you will have to be in Bombay by tomorrow morning. I'm not sure exactly how much you know about all this. Zal and Perin respect all our rites and customs, of course, but they have never had any deep religious feeling and my impression is that you haven't been greatly involved in that side of their life. There is something really difficult to be made clear. Zal is going to make all the decisions and he intends to be rigidly

158

orthodox. You as a non-Parsi, Ann, may well be kept at a distance in all this. I mean that quite literally. During the actual rites, you may only be allowed to hear what is said but not to sit close to the priests or see what is happening. That is going to be very hard to cope with." Freni's determinedly brisk voice shook a little, "You do understand what happens at a Parsi funeral, don't you?"

Ann stared at her aghast. Sam had once, somewhat defensively, told her about the Parsi custom of exposing their dead to vultures in high buildings known as Towers of Silence. "It isn't some perverse custom peculiar to us. Tibetans do a similar thing. They call it a sky burial." He had been dismissive of her horror at the idea. "It isn't any worse than what happens with Christian burial. The thought of being put into the ground gives *me* the shivers. Zoroastrians respect all the elements and don't like the idea of polluting earth, air, fire or water and we have found a practical way of dealing with that."

At that time, in the very early days of their getting to know one another, all this had seemed academic, remote, like hearing about some legendary, ancient behaviour and, in the onward rush of their life, it had never been relevant. It wasn't something she had wanted to dwell on. There had been no deaths in the family all this time to bring it home to her and she had let it slip from her conscious mind. Now, everything she had been told flooded back and her body was convulsed by something akin to an electric shock.

"No! Freni, no!" It was almost a scream. "No! No! My darling Sam. I can't bear it. My beautiful Sam." She subsided in a storm of weeping.

Freni tried to embrace her but she was pushed aside.

"No! Sam! You are so beautiful. I love you. It's horrible. They can't. They can't."

She was shivering uncontrollably, her shoulders heaved, tears poured down her red, distorted face and she was thumping her clenched hands on her chair. Bob was horrified by this disintegration of his composed, self-possessed friend.

"Stay with her, Bob. I'm going to call our doctor. He lives very nearby and fortunately it's a Sunday. He should be at home and able to get here quickly." Freni went out into the hall. When the doctor arrived, less than ten minutes later, Ann was sitting with her knees drawn up to her chest, her face buried in her ice-cold hands, still shivering. He put a gentle hand on her arm.

"Mrs Mehta, listen to me. I'm going to give you something to help you. An injection. Once I've given it, we can help you to your room. You will sleep for a while. You have to rest. You need to recover yourself. You will fall ill if you continue like this."

Ann made a visible effort. She sat straighter, wiped her face with her sleeve, took long shuddering breaths and within a few seconds was able to look directly at him.

"No, Doctor. Give me a moment. I'll get myself together. Freni, Bob, I'm sorry that I'm giving you all this trouble. Doctor, I mustn't sleep. I have to get to Bombay. I can't..." her voice failed but she quickly rallied, "I can't let Sam go and not be there."

Tears were falling but she was steadier. The doctor took her hand and felt her pulse.

"Very well. Naturally we don't want you to undergo further distress of any kind. I will just check you over. Then I will give you a mild sedative. Something that may make you a little drowsy, a little easier, but that won't incapacitate you."

"Come." Freni helped Ann to stand. "I'll take you and Ann to her room, Doctor."

The three of them went upstairs and after ten minutes, Freni returned and came over to Bob who had slumped exhaustedly into a chair.

"Ann is calmer but the doctor insists on sitting with her for a while to be sure that she's alright, so I can leave her with him for now. You have been wonderful, Bob. I feel so guilty. I had completely forgotten about your wife. Is she seriously injured? Is she in danger?"

"No. She seems to have been extremely lucky. She has a broken rib, leg and wrist and has bad cuts and bruises but nothing life threatening. I must get to her though. She is in shock and the doctors are concerned about her state of mind. She has no one else here in India and really needs me to be with her."

"What flight do you plan to take?"

"Ann and I are already booked on one at seven o'clock this evening. I got my people to arrange it but I wanted to give Ann as much time as possible."

"Could you get me on the flight? I'm sure that your officials could. Otherwise, Rustam can probably pull some strings. Fortunately, he is at home today and I've been quickly talking things over with him."

"How can you come to Bombay? That would be asking too much of you. It wouldn't be fair to your husband? You mustn't worry. I'll take care of Ann."

"Rustam spends so much time with his business that he expects me to live my own life anyway and, in this case, he fully agrees that I should come. He sees the situation as I do. We have only known Ann a short time but we are both greatly attached to her. In Bombay she will be afloat on a sea of difficulty. I see myself as a life raft. Think about it. She cannot possibly be alone in her own flat. She can't stay with you because of the complication of your wife's involvement." They looked straight at each other for a moment. "Jess is her dearest friend and in that she faces an added blow from which we want to shield her for as long as possible. As to Zal and Perin, there will have been reservations over this marriage and it will not be easy for them all to be together after what has happened. It was clear to me when I spoke to him, that Zal is in no mood to make any concessions to Ann. Whatever affection he has for her, he obviously believes that, because of her, Sam failed his community in life and is insisting that in death he should follow a strictly orthodox path. You have seen, and possibly share, Ann's revulsion at what will happen to Sam. She will certainly feel an outsider at our very ancient rites and will be denied a familiar and comforting farewell to him. She needs someone and somewhere neutral in all this. My unmarried sister has a flat in Bombay. Ann and I can stay there. Then, immediately after the funeral is over, I can insist on bringing Ann back here away from it all. Rustam is calling her mother now and will invite her to stay also. We will press her to come to us and be with Ann, to help her to recover and decide what she will do next. If she wants to return to England then they can go back together."

The force of Freni's personality and her clear-sighted planning would have carried the day but it all came to nothing. After the doctor left, Ann, unable to eat anything solid, managed some soup prepared for her and lay down to rest for a while, saying that she would pack a bag later. It seemed that a combination of medication and innate courage would see her through, but when Freni returned to see if she needed any help, she found her standing beside her bed looking at an untidy heap of clothes.

"I'm not sure what I have to do with these. There are so many." Putting her hand to her head, Ann closed her eyes and swayed dangerously. "Am I supposed to be packing these things? Where are we going? I thought we'd just come back. I can't seem to think."

"Don't worry just now. We'll do it later. Lie down again." Freni swept the clothes off the bed and put them on a chair. The doctor was recalled and a further, stronger sedative was given. They were all concerned about the effect on Ann of not going to Bombay. They were sure, however, that she was quite unequal to doing so. Either way it would end badly. There was no painless solution.

FIFTEEN

It was late afternoon the following day before Ann was fully awake. Freni had slept in her room all night, was back with her for most of the morning and on hand later to help her through a terrible moment of realisation. She would never see Sam again. She had failed to meet the last claim that he would ever make on her. She could not stop weeping, but her mini-breakdown seemed to have burned out the frantic horror and anguish that had gripped her. These were desolate but less desperate tears.

Freni held her hand for a time before saying, "Your mother is coming. We called her yesterday. Rustam has asked an associate in London to make the arrangements for her and to send a driver to get her to the airport. She will be here the day after tomorrow. You must both stay as long as you need to. You should take time to decide what you want to do next."

"You are so good to me." Despite her genuine gratitude, Ann spoke in a dreary monotone.

Edna, when she arrived, was equally grateful to their hosts but not entirely happy about accepting all this help and hospitality.

"It just doesn't feel right to me, Ann. After all, this is the first time that I've met them. Of course, you are obviously all very fond of each other but they are strangers to me."

Ann, though held in an imprisoning concentration of sorrow, did catch and understand the note of faint jealousy in her mother's voice. She roused herself to explain that this warm, open-hearted involvement in other people's lives – at the plus end of a sliding scale of interest and interference – was simply one of the features of Indian life and, moreover, that even their own comfortable circumstances had not prepared them for the level of affluence and influence that Rustam and Freni took for granted.

"They are really much wealthier than anyone we've ever had anything to do with. They certainly don't find it any hardship to do all this for us but the important thing is that it isn't a mere matter of giving what they can well afford. This isn't material generosity, it is generosity of spirit and that's what is so lovely about them."

Edna, already less prone to prescriptive attitudes after her first Indian experience, was won over by this. She had also learned to be more forthcoming, speaking unusually freely of her own heartbreak over Sam and, drawing an unaccustomed solace from physical contact, they held each other close.

For the next few days, Ann was treated as an invalid. Her passivity was as alarming as her previous, brief delirium. She did everything that they suggested. There was nothing that she wanted to do. Nothing that she did mattered. She was encouraged to spend her mornings on the wide, shaded verandah overlooking the huge garden, wrapped in a shawl and reading a book. Though planted luxuriantly with bougainvillea and hibiscus, this garden also had a stretch of cool grass, kept fresh and green through the efforts of three thin, leathery, cotton-clad gardeners with hoses and watering cans, which made for a tranquil view. Books, too, were always a consolation and these retreats eased her but, without warning, she would often find her face wet with tears that flowed without her volition or control. Nevertheless, a fragile peace was achieved and Edna was encouraged to leave her and go off for short outings with Freni to see something of Delhi.

"You need some breaks, Edna." Freni was not troubled by the fact that she was talking to Ann's mother. "It's probably best to leave Ann alone for short periods. She needs time and silence to deal with what has happened. She has lost so much. It's a terrible tragedy. But we both know that being young, she will eventually heal – at least partially. Of course this marriage was special. I don't want to offend you and I realise that all your instincts as parents led you and your husband to deplore it, but such opposition made it a matter of her and Sam against the world. That will make recovery much harder but she will recover. People do."

Edna, though she secretly could not disagree with this view of things and had seen all the special hazards of her daughter's marriage from the start, was taken aback by this cool forthrightness but, like Ann, found it impossible to be offended by Freni. She was surprised by how little difference culture made to the essence of a person and how, as with Perin, she was finding this elegant and sophisticated Parsi woman a sympathetic companion who shared many of her thoughts and feelings. This temporary lull was disturbed by the arrival of a letter from Bob.

Dear Freni,

I hope that Ann isn't suffering too much because she wasn't able to be at Sam's funeral. Her mother should be there by now and, when Ann is better, they will probably come to Bombay to settle her affairs. You and I do not know each other well but have shared a harrowing experience. I saw then how much you care about Ann and it will help you to know the situation here. There is quite a bit of gossip going round. Sam and Jess were seen together at the beach bungalow on the Saturday afternoon. This, in itself, might not have caused much comment but it did not look good for them to be driving back to the city at such an odd hour. Jess has been frank with me and, while I feel unable to go into details about what occurred between them, it is, as we feared, something that poses a further and serious threat to Ann's peace of mind. I am sending Jess back to England immediately on medical grounds so that there will be no question of their meeting each other. I feel that this would be too much for both of them. My superiors are not at all happy about our questionable involvement in the death of a local resident and insist that I should be swiftly transferred. Jess and I will manage to get through this crisis somehow and she will eventually join me in my new posting. We have been close to Sam and Ann for a long time and been a support to Ann in many situations. She would normally turn to us when in trouble. Instead she will lose Jess, *her dearest friend, in shadowy circumstances. I can hardly bear to think of what she has to go through. It will be impossible to keep all this from her but I am sure that you and her mother will break it to her in the best way you can. I took it on myself to contact her college superior, a Sister Frances, who will be writing to Ann. She is prepared to make arrangements that mean Ann will be able to return to her work should she wish to do so. All her other friends send their condolences and best wishes and will rally round her for as long as they are needed, though we all realise that Ann may very well decide to return to England. You and I will not have a chance to meet again and that is a matter for regret. My best wishes to you and your husband. Bob.*

"What do you think?" Freni looked anxiously at Edna after handing her the letter. "Should we tell Ann about this now or wait until she is stronger?"

"We must tell her. I don't know whether it is merely the effect of the sedation but she seems to have shut down at the moment and everything seems to just float over her. If we wait until she is more herself it might be harder for her *and* set her back. Better to get it over with."

"You've met Jess. Can you believe that there was anything between her and Sam? When Perin first called me about Ann's visit, she hinted that there were minor problems that she and Sam were struggling with but surely nothing like that. I got no sense of it from talking to Ann."

"Jess was almost certainly attracted to Sam. I tried to warn Ann when I was staying with her but maybe I was too cautious and did not make myself plain enough. None of them, not even Bob, seemed to see it. I can't.... I don't believe that Sam reciprocated in any way. But they were alone together that night and she is a very fetching little thing, with a habit of getting what she wants. You can see what might be possible in a situation like that. If what Bob suggests did happen, then I know that Sam would have been appalled at what he had done. I have no doubt of his strong feelings for Ann or of his essential decency." She broke off sharply, recalling what was lost and all the suffering left behind.

On being told what Bob had written and understanding all that this implied, Ann was not overcome but galvanised. She was flooded by a fury that washed away all her apathy and temporarily assuaged her pain. In Jess she had a more tangible target than mere fate for the rage that already underpinned her misery. She insisted that she and Edna should return at once to Bombay. Clearly her absence from Sam's funeral would only have fuelled the gossip that Bob wrote about. If she was back in her flat and carrying on her life there, it might silence some of this. She could, she would, be seen with Zal and Perin. There was, after all, one last thing she could do for Sam. She could outface any doubts about him and demonstrate total commitment to his memory, respect for his religion and closeness to his family.

"I just can't deal with Ann at the moment." Edna came to Freni looking exhausted. "After all these days in a kind of torpor, she's suddenly full of rage and an almost hysterical urge to act. I understand her anger but this sudden hyperactivity doesn't seem normal. Do you think she's fit to go to Bombay?"

"In this situation, Edna, how on earth can we judge what is normal? A period of torpor was a necessary respite but she can't take tranquillisers forever and she has to face an enormous amount of pain. Her rage and rush of activity seem to me ways in which she is dealing with that, survival strategies if you like. You'll need to keep watch for signs that she might collapse again but, yes, I think you should go to Bombay."

Four days later, back at the flat, Kishen opened the door and stood in front of them, his head bowed and his hands folded in the respectful Hindu salutation. There were tears in his eyes but he behaved with his usual impeccable dignity.

"Welcome home, Memsahib. I am feeling such deep sorrow for Sahib and I am here only to serve you."

Ann's lip trembled and she had to resist an urge to hug him, knowing that this would profoundly shock him.

"Thank you, Kishen. Thank you for taking care of everything all this time. I am lucky to have you here."

She walked blindly past him into the awaiting emptiness. Edna, after a brief greeting, hurried in after her.

"I'll ask Kishen to bring some tea," she said briskly, "and then we'll unpack and get organised so that we are quite ready for your in-laws. It will be a little tiring seeing them after the journey but I can see that it is something that you need to do as soon as possible. So! Let's get on with things."

Zal and Perin had been invited for dinner but had opted for a short visit in the early evening instead. It was a difficult meeting, only partly tempered by Edna's presence. Perin, though pale and tired, was relatively unchanged but Zal looked smaller, frailer, did not burst into immediate, assertive speech and was uncharacteristically subdued throughout.

"You must be bitterly hurt that I wasn't here for ...." Ann's voice broke, "for Sam's funeral. Is there anything I can do now? I feel strongly that we have to be seen to mourn Sam together."

Perin went to her and put her arms round her. "You are very right. We have to forget everything that has happened and only remember our dearest Sam." She had to pause briefly. "I know that he tried to live a life with you that put aside many of our ways. He feared that they might come between you." Again she had to stop and control her voice. "We can't blame you for that. We don't blame you for that." She shot a fierce look at Zal. "I don't want to upset you by speaking of distressing things but it is our custom to burn a lamp and put fresh flowers in our home for nine days after our dear ones are taken from us. Tomorrow is the ninth day. You should bring the flowers and sit with me for a time. That should be a comfort to you. People everywhere like to offer flowers to lost loved ones." She patted Ann's arm. "Our family has already met together for prayers and to make gifts to charity. We shall do this twice more in a formal way and you should be with us. It is our belief that Sam's spirit will see us and be pleased by our good words, good thoughts and good deeds, for these three things are a very important part of our religious duty."

Ann believed that Perin was right about Sam's motive in keeping their marriage free of all the religious elements of his heritage though, in their first weeks together in Cambridge, he had been anxious that she should understand exactly who and what he was and willing, even keen, to talk about such things. He had shown her photographs and booklets and she recalled pictures of priests in long, white robes, white caps and white face masks. It had all been fascinating but had seemed remote from her immediate concerns or interests. They had both been so totally absorbed in their emotions, in a campaign to survive as a couple that they had isolated themselves from so much. She now saw how unthinking that attitude had been, how much she and Sam had missed by ignoring this rich tradition, but she put a stop to such thoughts. They felt like a criticism of Sam who could not now defend himself and she was absolutely clear that no better understanding of his religion would have reconciled her to that last unimaginable act in the Tower of Silence. She had to use every ounce of willpower to shut out appalling images that threatened to make thinking of Sam unendurable. Chilling thoughts of the brutalities that burial inflicts on the body, ignominies for which the idea of an enduring soul seemed inadequate consolation, had assailed her at her father's graveside, but that churchyard scene, so often encountered in books, films and life, had been imprinted on her as normal. It was one of the rituals that people use to protect themselves from nightmares. She had forfeited any such relief here, lost that shield and was face to face with a stark reality.

Over the next few days, Edna, seeing Ann regaining command of herself, beginning to deal with matters awaiting her attention, kept in the background as far as possible, ready to help but trying not to interfere. On one front, however, she did make a stand, pushing strongly for Ann to return with her to England.

"What will you do here without Sam? You will be horribly lonely. You have done well to fit in as you have, but this is still a foreign country. If you come back you will lose five years of your life but you will regain over twenty. You are still young. You can build a new future on those early years, all those childhood experiences. Please come home."

As she had been over her marriage, Ann was deaf to her mother's warnings and pleas. She clung to the task she had set herself of creating a personal, living memorial to Sam.

"I can't come. You should understand. After father's death you felt that coming with me to India would be disloyal – and you were only coming for a few weeks. For me to leave now, forever, would be a betrayal. I owe it to Sam to base any future I have on what we managed to make of our life together here."

Having seen how tenacious and obstinate Ann could be, Edna gave up all efforts to make her change her mind. They seemed to be re-enacting an earlier confrontation, with Ann once more determined on a risky and unwise course. She felt a weary resignation and decided that she could do little more to help. Begging Ann to at least promise to come for a visit very soon, she booked her own flight to London. This time she was confident enough to travel without any companion. She felt some regrets for, though India would always be an alien place that meant little to her, she had forged alliances and friendships in her brief stays here and it was sad to feel that these were over. During this visit, she had seen little of Perin. They had exchanged a few words when in company with Ann but their previous understanding seemed forgotten. She had barely spoken to Zal, once so enthusiastically her guide to Bombay. She understood how it was for both of them. They had certainly pitied her and Clifford for, in effect, losing a child. Now, seeing her with Ann could only be a harsh reminder that they were the ones to have suffered the irretrievable loss. On the day of her departure, they phoned to wish her a safe journey but it was a brief call and she and Ann went alone to the airport.

"Promise me that you will come to see me as soon as you possibly can. I shall be so worried about you. Your grandparents would be relieved to see you after all that you have been through. I realise that we are a staid and unemotional lot in comparison to what you have grown used to but they love you and miss you. Don't forget us all completely."

Ann had tears in her eyes. "I'm sorry Mother. I know that you have had more than your share of suffering too. Just try to understand. I don't want to make you unhappy but I have to do this. I will come as soon as I have settled everything and can fit a visit in around whatever work I manage to continue. Give my love to everyone and say that I will see them soon."

Once again Edna, walking away to the boarding gate, turned and gave her a long look as if she hoped to convey all the emotions that she still found impossible to put into words.

SIXTEEN

Her mother's departure left Ann unprotected from the loneliness of the flat. She dealt with this by keeping up a rigorous discipline. Every morning, unrested and heavy-eyed, with a weight in the pit of her stomach at the thought of the day ahead, she forced herself to bath, dress and breakfast at her normal times. Kishen's daytime presence was some comfort. It did not help that, while he too maintained his regular habits, his face had lost its gentle cheerfulness and was pinched and dejected, but they did offer each other wordless support. A mutual affection had developed within their very unequal relationship. There was something admirable, endearing, about this loyal servant, with his pride in service, his readiness to identify with the household in which he worked and his willingness to weave his own life and feelings into its fabric. For now, he provided her only bearable human contact.

She had seen none of her friends. Any suggestion of contact with them led to thoughts of Jess, arousing a ferment of misery and bitterness that left her tremulous and sick. Though she went to one or two formal dinners at Dahanipur House, she refused all invitations to family meals. She could endure being there when surrounded by other people but to be alone with her in-laws without such a safety barrier was beyond her.

Every evening, after her simple supper, Kishen would come and ask her if she needed anything further and then retire to his quarters. She wanted to be alone with her memories of Sam but found herself alone with her agonised longings. Part of her saw this suffering as a kind of gift to him but the harder element of her character fought against it and, as so often, she turned to books. Sam had possessed a collection of thrillers that she had never looked at and, one evening, she started to read one of his favourites. The gripping impetus of the storytelling gave her a temporary respite, but there was no prolonged escape. She heard Sam's voice, loving, light and amused, "I just hope that you aren't going to see our life as a succession of literary genres." Blinded with tears, she gave up and went to bed. When lying down, at least her body got some rest.

Since the day that she had returned from Delhi, she had slept on the single bed in the study, using the main bedroom only as a dressing room but one sleepless night, she went in and lay down on Sam's side of their bed, with her face buried in his pillow as if she could somehow conjure up his physical presence. There was only the continued chill cruelty of his absence that left her wretched and bone-tired. By the next morning, however, she had regained her self-control. She knew that to survive, she had to make a determined effort to restart her life.

She began by ringing several friends. She excused herself from entertaining at home for the present but said that she would like to see them again and an evening get-together with many of the regular group was arranged. Next, she went to meet her teaching superior.

Sister Frances had large, round, pale brown eyes that Jess had once unkindly likened to overcooked poached eggs. She always wore plain, white, cotton saris and beige sandals that merged with the light brown of her feet so that, as Jess had again remarked, she seemed to be growing out of the dust of India. Ann now deeply regretted having encouraged what seemed, in these changed circumstances, like casual disrespect. She was moved by this kindly woman's strenuous efforts to accommodate her within the life of the college and to help her in every possible way. Her lack of formal qualifications had posed problems but all the staff had been impressed by her earlier work and her undoubted rapport with her students, and they had all eventually agreed that she should be offered extended teaching hours. She gratefully accepted these. The term was well underway but Sister Frances had made provision for the extra classes within the timetable and had to date used these periods for a series of special lectures. It had all been dealt with efficiently. Ann could begin work almost immediately. Her days would once more have a structure that she could cling to.

The evening with her friends was testing. Before leaving home, she looked at herself in the mirror, once again dressed for a party, and was seized by such a spasm of grief that she almost telephoned to say that she was unable to make it. She stared at the paler, thinner face confronting her and straightened her shoulders. She could not hide away forever. It wasn't a case of waiting until she was ready for this. She would never be ready – but it had to be done at some point. Telling herself that she was lucky to be meeting friends who could be trusted to behave with warmth and sensitivity, she left the flat before she had a chance to falter. She was greeted without undue fuss. Everyone spoke naturally and affectionately of Sam but carefully avoided any mention of Bob and Jess, whose absence shouted out at her, making this silence worse than any comment or discussion would have been.

She had realised that meeting Hari was inevitable and guilt over her past behaviour made her dread this but he made things easy for her.

"There is nothing I can say, Ann. What has happened is beyond words. I can only ask you to always look on me as a friend. Unfortunately, I can't stay this evening. I have to attend a business dinner. I came by to see you and to say that you can call on me at any time if there is anything I can do to help."

He chatted briefly to the others and, with a tact she appreciated, said goodbye and left.

Having crossed this barrier, she made a determined effort to see her in-laws more often but was dismayed to find that much of the goodwill built up between them had dissipated and that Zal had completely changed. His confident volubility had gone and he rarely spoke directly to her.

Perin was frank. "You must forgive Zal. You know what it is to lose a father and a husband. We are learning what it is to lose a son. Until I spoke of them recently, you won't have realised that our Zoroastrian beliefs are important to me. I am a simple person and have always had time to remember all that I was taught as a child. Those things give me some comfort. There is no comfort for Zal. He is clever. All he ever wanted was to be successful. For that he broke away from his family and his childhood. He has always been taken up by his work and has forgotten everything else. There is nothing to help him. His position, his money, all the things that he believed to be of first importance, are nothing to him just now."

"Zal has no need of my forgiveness. I know exactly how he feels. I can't find comfort anywhere either. Without Sam nothing seems to matter much to me. But I still love Sam and I will make something matter. I won't throw away my life because that would be to belittle what he has lost. Zal will also manage to carry on. And there is Cyrus. His medical training has taken so long but he will soon be back and he will give Zal something to be proud of, to care about."

"You are very right. Cyrus will certainly help to bring him back to himself. But there will always be something missing in his life."

"And he won't want me around too often as a reminder of that." Ann's voice was unsteady. "You must both feel that if Sam had not met me, if he had married one of your own, none of this would have happened."

For the first time since Ann had met her, Perin burst into tears. "I too made it happen. If only I hadn't thought of your going to Delhi. If only you had been here with him. Oh, my dear son. He was such a good, sweet boy. I only wanted him to be happy." She could not speak for weeping.

"Perin," Ann's voice was soft, "when we met I said that we had one thing in common – we both loved Sam. What we have in common now is remorse for what we have done to him. The only way we can make amends is by carrying on living as bravely as possible."

"You are a dear girl. You are very right. We have all done things that should have been done better. Sam too, on that night, made a dreadful…."

"Don't, Perin! You can blame me, blame yourself, Jess, God, Fate. Don't ever blame Sam. Like all of us, he must have been driven by feelings he couldn't control and he is the one who has paid heavily for all our mistakes. Don't think of holding him to account."

Worn out by her efforts and drained by these emotional encounters, Ann was relieved to start at the college. Anxious to justify Sister Frances's faith in her and worried about her fitness for what was a more serious job than she had previously held, she spent many evenings preparing teaching notes and materials and, in those hours of quiet concentration, finally found some release. She was surprised, guiltily surprised, as she came to the end of her first year, to find that in the classes themselves she was recovering a capacity for actual enjoyment. She had intended to be active, to be positive but to feel even the slightest happiness so soon seemed shallow and unforgiveable.

Freni had phoned frequently throughout the year for, though she was anxious to come to Bombay, she led a very busy life and only finally arrived the following March. She based herself at her sister's flat but spent much of her time with Ann, occasionally staying with her overnight. She proved to be a determined antidote to such negative thinking.

"I don't want to hear this nonsense," she spoke as usual, forcefully. "You will grieve for Sam for a long time. Losing him has scarred your life. But you are young. You can't cut yourself off from every natural feeling. Sam loved you. Would he ask you to do that? It isn't as if this pleasure you feel so bad about was in partying or frivolity. It is in finding something serious and useful to do. Far from feeling guilty, you should feel proud. We are all proud of you," she paused and her face darkened. "All except Zal perhaps. He is behaving outrageously. He has always seen himself as the fixed centre of the universe. God knows what Perin has had to put up with all these years. I can't help feeling sorry for him though. He has had a sharp lesson and found out that he can't control everything, that he is not superman; but he is acting as if no one but himself has suffered in all this. He is punishing you for that and cutting you out of his life. And I suspect that he is insisting that Perin draws back too. It's disgraceful."

Ann, recalling her own response to an earlier bereavement, could not blame Zal but did not reveal this as she would only provoke strong reproof and condemnation for too much soul searching. She was finding ways to deal with Freni's often unsparing frankness but was mostly grateful for her outspokenness. She refused to allow any reminders of Jess to surface, only too glad to have such a second chance at friendship.

"It's good to have you here Freni. You always see things as they are and you aren't afraid to speak out about anything. You help me so much."

"I'll speak about one other thing. I never wanted babies. They are disruptive, messy and inconvenient creatures, even in India where we get so much help with them. Now, without any of that trouble, I've been given the gift of a daughter. That's what you are to me Ann."

Ann hugged her but these words brought on a bout of self-castigation. She should visit her mother. Edna wrote less frequently these days. She understood that a permanent job was a necessary part of a viable life for Ann and that having one would make it more complicated for her to come home, but when she did write, her letters were increasingly reproachful in tone, referring bluntly to broken promises. Ann knew that she had temporised too long. She forced herself to forget the cold fact that Sam had never had his English family Christmas and set herself to sending a positive reply.

Bombay
25/5/72

Mother,

I'm sorry you feel that I'm neglecting you. I do want to come home but it has been difficult. My work is very important to me and it isn't just the hours that I spend in college that keep me occupied but those I have to spend in preparation. I told you that Sister Frances had booked me on various courses to boost my qualifications and how they have taken up a lot of otherwise free time. I had to do a lot of studying during vacations. That's nearly over. I could come home in December. I'd love to be there for Christmas with the whole family. You know that people celebrate here but it never seems right when it is sunny and hot. It feels fake somehow. It would be good to enjoy the real thing again. I know that Christmas seems a long way off but it will come on us very quickly. Sam and I once talked about how weirdly time behaves. At first after he died, every day seemed to drag on forever. It sometimes felt as if they would never end. Now, they have somehow speeded up. It is hard to believe that I have been on my own for a year and a half. It has been difficult but I am really trying to be busy and positive. Coming home will be part of that. Let me know what the family is planning. Will you be spending Christmas Day at the farm? Give my love to Grandpa and Grandma and to everyone and tell them that I am looking forward to seeing them all.

Ann.

Edna, obviously delighted to have a fixed date at last, began to write more regularly and her letters became more chatty and natural again. Glad to have pleased her, Ann also felt happier. She still had sleepless nights and nights when she woke from a fitful sleep to find her pillow wet with involuntary tears and, though she kept herself occupied most of the time, she often had to get through many dreary daytime hours, but life was slowly reclaiming her and she was increasingly willing to be reclaimed. She was being truthful in saying that she was looking forward to Christmas at home but she was not entirely sure about meeting the family en masse. She believed them to have deplored her marriage. How would they react now that it had ended so badly and she was a widow? It wasn't an agreeable thought. She found that the doubts that had been holding her back so long were again plaguing her. Then a letter from her grandfather brought all these considerations to an end.

Long Meadow Farm
20/11/72

Dear Ann,

I'm writing to prepare you for a shock when you arrive next month. Your mother has refused to tell you that

she is very unwell. She is not behaving like her normal self in believing that you should not be told. I think that for a long time she hoped that it would not be necessary, that this was a minor problem and that she would recover before you came home. It turns out that she was being unrealistic about this and I have been forced to override her. You have to know what is happening. Though she did not tell us either, she has apparently been worried about her health for some time and done nothing about it. Then, just over a month ago, she suffered sudden and dramatic symptoms and was diagnosed with cancer...ovarian cancer. I don't like to give you this news after all that you have been through but it was too late to operate and, though she is undergoing treatment, things don't look good. You know your mother. She isn't one to make a fuss. The good thing is that she will see you and that this makes her happy whatever fears she has. You have much of her grit and determination and we count on you to get through yet another ordeal bravely for her sake. She has moved in with us and you too will stay here. Your grandma and I are both sorry that you were not told all this earlier. We will both be very glad to see you. It has been too long and we have missed you.
Grandpa.

"The good thing is that she will see you." These words leapt out at Ann and, together with the news that her mother was no longer in her own home, made her realise exactly how bad things were, just what she had to face up to and how much she had to reproach herself for.

There was another wearisome flight home and, not long after a Christmas very different from the one that she had looked forward to, another funeral. Once more they all assembled in their little church, filed between the worn gravestones and stood next to Clifford's grave at the place now neatly prepared for Edna. There were no birds and no sunshine this time. It was sleety and cold. The ground was frozen. It all seemed to reflect Ann's condition. She only got through it all because, exhausted by shock after shock, she was in a kind of emotional coma.

Practical matters had to be dealt with, however, and she called up sufficient resolve and mental energy to deal with those. Once again she had to call on the forbearance of Sister Frances and take extra leave. Her mother had left everything to her and now their cottage was hers but she simply did not have the courage to enter it. She felt that, no matter how stoical they were, she could not ask her grandparents to sort through her mother's possessions and she turned to her cousin Charles, asking him to enlist the help of their cleaner to dispose of any clothing or other sundries. If he boxed up and stored everything else, she would eventually summon the will to deal with it. She promised to return at some unspecified time and get to grips with everything. Meanwhile, she put the management of the cottage into the hands of their family solicitor with instructions to rent it out for her. She recoiled from the idea of being in it but could not bring herself to put it up for sale. It wasn't merely an asset. It was the embodiment of her childhood.

Her grandparents did not comment on any of her decisions. Though they carried on quietly with their household tasks and the work of the farm, they had lost their brisk efficiency and several times she saw them standing together, their hands clasped, looking out towards the church. Her relations and friends were kind but remote as if only too aware that it was only after her marriage that her family had been plunged into tragedy. Their normal taciturnity had never indicated any lack of self-possession or poise but now when she was with them they were ill at ease. They no longer counted on a common language with her. It was as if they began by seeing her as Ann Baker only to be constrained by the presence of Ann Mehta. Her sense that Edna's visit to Bombay had bridged the gulf between her two worlds had been an illusion. She was keen to leave as soon as possible. All her being, all her thoughts were fiercely directed towards her life in India. Her commitment to that as a memorial to Sam was all that she had left.

SEVENTEEN

Zal and Perin met Ann at the airport. They were shocked into greater warmth than they had shown of late. Zal still said very little and made a great to-do of taking charge of her suitcases but Perin held her tightly for a moment and, standing back to look at her, held on to both her hands.

"So much sorrow, Ann. You have had so much sorrow. I know you felt very alone after your father died but, thanks God, I can share memories of your mother with you. She and I had such good talks when she was here for her first visit. You are right to come back to us. We are your family now."

This renewed closeness proved to be very fragile. Although their relationship appeared less fraught and Ann once again frequently visited Dahanipur House, she could not shake off a sense of underlying tension. Sam was always in their minds. She had become reliant on the understanding that had grown up between herself and Perin but began to suspect that her mother-in-law had disguised a far greater awareness of their difference than she had realised. This had not been obvious while Sam was alive but, clearly, as his wife, she had enjoyed an acquired legitimacy which, as his widow, she seemed largely to have lost. There was an element of fairness in this. She had conformed, adopted the externals of Indian life and learned enough of the country's history and politics to discuss its affairs intelligently but, though intrigued by, even enchanted by, its internal rhythms, her secret heart, while sometimes afflicted by arrhythmic flutters, had stubbornly maintained a slow, remembered beat. She turned away from this disturbing insight and looked to her dedication to Sam for a reason to carry on here however lonely or out of place she sometimes felt.

She slipped back into her Indian ways as if floating out into a warm pool. There was nothing beyond her fixed timetable, these created habits, this willed existence. She had friends close enough to make being with them agreeable, but not so close as to threaten her equanimity if they failed her in any way. She recognised the aridity at the heart of this and tried to forget the enveloping warmth she had known when Jess was always there for her. About a month after Sam's death, she had received a letter from Bob in which he said how sorry he was that their friendship had ended as it had and how much he missed her but that it was probably impossible for them to keep in touch. He had not mentioned Jess. Losing his solid, reassuring presence in the background of her life was an added deprivation and she frequently had to call up all her latent outrage to beat back desolation. Though she regularly met Hari in the company of their other friends, he was quieter, more subdued and no longer singled her out or talked to her in the same way as before. He clearly shared her regret for their previous light- hearted flirtation and she understood his withdrawal but was irrationally upset by it.

Her work progressed. Sister Frances continued to encourage her to use any time outside her teaching for further part-time courses. The intellectual rigour of her girlhood was proving valuable and she managed these with ease but it was very hard, after the respite of lively academic days, to step into the flat and face her solitary nights.

She had fiercely and finally wiped her mind of the images that had tormented her after Sam's funeral and, to offset these, had kept his photographs all around to help her to hold on to him, alive and beautiful. From one of these he looked out at her with bright, eager eyes, a twelve year old boy, no longer connected to the traditional world of his grandfather, the old India where he was born but, even within the urban neutrality his father had chosen for him, still strongly held by custom and history. A pang of love that was almost maternal shook her. Meeting her, he had moved so much further away from that history and how badly those hopeful eyes had been betrayed. She was filled with a yearning for him that she managed to suppress while she was involved with work or friends but which was always ready to stab her during these moments of lonely homecoming. She had to fight a hunger to be held and kissed, to feel his warm, urgent body close to her. Worse, in its way, was her longing to rest on a strong shoulder and feel all this misery and tension drain from her. That was over.

There was fortunately always study, marking student essays or preparation for the day ahead to engage and distract her. She never ceased to be grateful for Kishen who had completely taken over the running of the flat and the provision of food and other requirements of daily life. This, her only home, was a sorrowful, haunted place but his unobtrusive yet supportive presence made it a little less so.

She spent her first Christmas vacation after Edna's death in Delhi with Freni who, recognising just how grim an anniversary this was and recollecting what other associations might trouble Ann, treated her with more overt tenderness than usual.

"I won't ask if you are happy, Ann. But are you settled? Are you satisfied with what you are doing?"

"Most of the time I get by. Occasionally it's better than that, because I do enjoy my work. I am often very lonely but I rush into doing something and I get over it."

"I have to say that we Parsis are great believers in activity, in getting down to it. It's what makes many of us do so well in life and why we play such a big role in this country despite our small numbers. Perhaps you have learned something from us!"

"I have to put in a word for my own ancestry. All my relations are equally energetic and hardworking though what they do is far less notable." She sighed. "Isn't it strange to find similarity where we expect to find difference? When I married Sam, I thought I was breaking away from familiar customs and habits but all that's happened is that we…" she stopped for a moment, "I… have been caught up in a new set. It's something that creeps up on you. Most of the time we live almost subconsciously. It's rather like digestion or breathing. We just carry on and we only think about what we are actually doing when something breaks down. That seems to be so wherever you are."

Freni had extolled the energy of the Parsis and she certainly demonstrated it. She did not allow any sadness to prevent them from enjoying all the usual partying. Life with her was fast paced, but there was always time to talk to each other in the unreserved way that had previously only been possible with Jess. Ann had to ignore incoherent thoughts of an old friend and concentrate on the pleasure of being with a new one. It was hard to leave Delhi and lose this lively companionship but she was due at the college in early January and, with sad recollections of her earlier return after Sam's death, went back to solitude, sobriety and the less salubrious climate of Bombay.

A few days after her return, she received a surprise telephone call from Hari. "Ann. Did you have a good holiday in Delhi? Look, I haven't asked you this before because I didn't think that it was appropriate but will you come out for dinner with me one evening?"

Ann did not answer for a considerable time. She was alarmed by the excitement that flooded through her at hearing his voice. She did not want to risk the equilibrium she held on to so carefully and he could easily become a disturbing factor in her life.

He seemed to understand this long silence. "There's no need to worry. It's just dinner with an old friend."

She realised that to refuse his invitation would be to make too much of it but she dreaded being seen out and about, enjoying herself with anyone. She knew that this was ridiculous. Whatever her concern over redeeming Sam in the eyes of the gossips, she wasn't a Victorian widow. She decided to compromise.

"Sorry. I'd like to see you. I don't really want to eat out anywhere though. Kishen is an excellent cook and he's had few chances to show what he can do for a very long time. Why don't you come here? The day after tomorrow? About seven thirty?"

"That would be very pleasant. Thank you. I'm sure that Kishen is an expert chef but it's good company more than good food that I'm looking forward to."

Ann regretted her invitation as soon as she had given it. This would be her first experience for a long time of being in male company and all her guilty feelings about Hari resurfaced. How could she be inviting him into the place where she and Sam had shared so much? She should not have considered being alone with him here. When she told Kishen to prepare for the proposed dinner, she said, "You always look after all our visitors perfectly but I want Chand Sahib to have a very good evening with us. I'd like you to stay on after dinner until he goes. I hope that won't be too late."

Kishen gave her a more direct look than usual. "Yes, Memsahib, I will wait. No matter what time. I will be here."

Her misgivings proved unnecessary. Hari was tactful and considerate, avoiding sensitive topics and keeping to current affairs and social and cultural events. Only as they grew more comfortable with each other again, did he turn to more personal matters. He asked about her teaching and had some useful advice on some of the problems she had to deal with and, for the first time, he told her about his business and how he was in the process of expanding it.

"It's a time consuming task. I sit for hours in dusty government offices with small men peering at me over teetering piles of papers and there is endless form filling involved. I sometimes feel like Houdini. I get tied up in this tangle of bureaucratic chains and ropes and because no-one can quite see how that is done, it's possible, with some ingenuity, some sleight of hand, to free myself without anyone being able to pin down exactly how I did it. Paradoxically, if there were fewer chains it would be harder to escape. People would follow what I was up to more easily. Does that shock you?"

"I suppose in a way it does but it shouldn't. It's all part of the same system that has made it possible for me to be doing what I'm doing. I got my job by unorthodox methods. I can only justify that by being really good at it – as I honestly think that I am."

"We'll make a full-blooded Indian of you yet." Hari spoke lightly and moved on to ask her what she had thought of a play that they had both seen. They had always found it easy to talk to each other and their conversation was so engrossing that they were surprised when they realised that it was past midnight.

"I must go." Hari stood up. "Thank you Ann. I hope that we can do this again very soon."

As they went into the hall, Kishen came out of the kitchen and went to open the door. Hari spoke to him in Hindi. "I don't believe that your memsahib usually keeps you up so late, Kishen. Thank you for a delicious meal, and for taking such care of me." He turned to Ann and finally allowed himself a flash of his former mischief. "I told you. You don't have to worry about meeting me. You are not in need of a bodyguard."

Before she could think of a suitable response, he had started off down the stairs without a backward glance.

The second time that he came to the flat, Hari did venture on a reference to Sam. "I understand how painful it must have been to deal with all the gossip that went around after Sam's accident. You are obviously wary of opening yourself to anything like that again but I honestly don't think that our eating out together occasionally will cause undue comment. I can't always accept your hospitality and because of her belief in the inadequacies of my bachelor arrangements, my mother insists on looking in on me every day and makes quite a production of any dinner I arrange, so it's probably best if you don't come to my place. I think going to a hotel or restaurant would be more practical."

Ann saw the sense of this. In a way, full of unexamined fears of the intimacy of the flat, she was glad to go out. She felt some qualms about the effects that this socialising might have on her in-laws but they never spoke of it. She was growing increasingly apart from them. The warmth that had flickered into life again after her return from England was fading and Zal and Perin had other matters to distract them.

After years of training and working abroad, Cyrus finally returned to Bombay and took a post as a surgeon at a major Bombay hospital. He was already seen as an important figure in his profession and his success invigorated his father, re-igniting something of Zal's old swagger and confidence. There were a number of elaborate parties at Dahanipur House at which Ann spent most of her time quietly talking to any lesser relatives present. She and Cyrus had a connection of a kind. They shared memories of Sam's graduation and Cyrus was now the only other person who had been at her Cambridge wedding, but this was not enough to bind them into any sort of friendship. Sam was disconcertingly between them and they felt the embarrassment that Cyrus's position as the surviving son and white hope of his father imposed on them.

Soon after his return, he announced his engagement to the daughter of a prominent Parsi businessman. There were formal exchanges of gifts between the two families, with much toing and froing between the couple's homes, and groups of excited Parsi ladies in beautiful, elaborate saris, fluttered from one to the other like clouds of migrating butterflies. Six months later there was a splendid wedding and, immersed in all the obligatory ceremonial that took place prior to this event, Perin, like Zal, regained much of her former energy. Cyrus had chosen well. His fiancée, Mehru, was well connected, good-looking, sophisticated and socially adept. At last his mother would have the daughter-in-law that she had always pictured.

The ceremony took place in the large courtyard of a popular venue with sufficient space to cater for hundreds of guests. It was very much a traditional affair in a traditional setting. Zal and Perin had gone there very early, leaving Ann to come later and, though they sent their car back for her, she faced walking into the gathering alone. She squared her shoulders, took a deep breath and went in. The first thing that she saw was a large central platform where white robed priests were standing beside two elaborately decorated chairs prepared for the bride and groom. Their families were sitting in a group to one side of these and, without thinking, having forgotten what Freni had once told her about her possible status in religious rites, she moved towards them. Perin's brother-in-law came over to her and took her arm.

"I'm sorry Ann but it is not proper for you to sit close to the priests. Come over here."

He led her to one of the rows of seats in the body of the courtyard and made a fuss of settling her comfortably there. She sat smiling at everyone but inwardly smarting and berating herself for exposing herself to humiliation. After the ceremony, she moved, still smiling, towards the far side of the courtyard and the long rows of tables prepared for the wedding dinner where many of the guests had quickly seated themselves. Bearers had already set out some food on the banana leaves that were the Indian version of disposable plates and were moving continuously up and down between the close-packed seats, calling out to people, "Bolo! Bolo!" "Speak up! Speak up!" ladling out additional helpings of curry or hot chapattis on request.

"Come here with us Ann. You should be with us."

Perin had been looking out for her and took her over to join the rest of the family. Ann appreciated this thoughtfulness and made an effort to join in all the exuberant chatter but, mingling with the crowd after the meal, her sociability concealed a hot, choked soreness in her chest as she suppressed ridiculous tears. Everyone must feel awkward with her. How could they fail to make a comparison between this unlucky, alien widow and the evening's glittering couple who fulfilled everyone's hopes and aspirations?

She had a wretched night dwelling on her loneliness, her isolation. She had never before looked so coolly at her position here. If Sam had lived, if they had eventually had children, she might have been unequivocally taken to the community's heart and have found it a true home – but she had no one. She belonged nowhere. An uncharacteristic self-pity overcame her. Yet, as always, by morning, her willpower proved stronger than her despair and she had pulled herself back from this dangerous cliff edge.

She spent another consoling Christmas with Freni. She loved Delhi. Its traffic might be equally undisciplined and noisy but it had a less frantic, more defined character than amorphous, cosmopolitan Bombay, something reminiscent of the unique atmosphere that made any English town distinct from every other. Where Bombay existed as a constructed entity, set apart on its islands, a city floating between sea and sky, Delhi gave her the feeling that it grew organically from the village life around it, a life that merged with its margins and blended into them. She particularly loved it in the winter. The cold, crisp weather was a delight after the sticky heat of Bombay. Just being able to put on her woollen skirts and wear a coat was a treat. Returning to the house after late afternoon outings, she would breathe in the fragrant smokiness from the hundreds of small fires being lit for evening cooking that wafted around and settled low over the city. It had the smell and feel of winter bonfires at home.

She was back in Bombay in January to start her college duties, the essential framework on which she had built her new life. She re-entered her sedate social round and continued to meet Hari who was rapidly becoming as trusted and congenial a friend as Freni. On leaving Delhi this time, though, there was a disconcerting change in her. This latest visit had only given her a very temporary break from the dissatisfactions she was trying to shake off. She was jaded and downhearted. Starting out in India had been so thrilling. It had been a great adventure – a passionate romance. Now, here she was, a thirty plus, practically spinsterish teacher, as settled in her ways as any Norfolk or Indian villager. Her sense of purpose, her commitment to living for Sam began to fray.

The monsoon had always been a trying time but this year the problems it gave rise to seemed unendurable. The sliding doors to the balcony had to be constantly closed against the rain that came almost horizontally across the sea, lashing the building and finding the slightest crack in walls or woodwork. Because it was impossible to completely dry anything out, everything in the flat took on a faint odour of mushrooms, shoes and belts acquired a greenish sheen and bath towels were always unpleasantly clammy. She herself never felt clean and fresh. She decided to install air conditioners. Not only would they overcome the problem of fungal damp, they would also cut out the noise that was increasingly maddening her.

In the last two years, new buildings had sprung up in every available space nearby and several attractive old bungalows had been demolished to make way for high-rise blocks. There were probably nearly as many people in the small area around her flat as in the whole of her home town and they made a considerable din. It began early with their ablutions. Her neighbours could be heard from open bathroom windows and their servants stood around in various compounds, holding small pots of water and brushing their teeth energetically. Everyone gargled and spat with enthusiasm and had an endless, versatile repertoire of throat cleansing routines, as if daily attempting to regurgitate the pollutants of their unclean city. Soon after this, the first of the usual hawkers began shrieking their ear-splitting descant above the throb and rumble of the everyday pandemonium and she grew more and more infuriated with the shrill, nasal whine of film music coming at her hour after hour from numerous cheap radios.

She told herself that she had to overcome her moodiness and bad temper. All her sustained efforts to fight despondence and stay positive would have been wasted if she did not carry on, but she could not shake off her discontent. The rewards of her work were becoming more a matter of course and nothing new and challenging seemed to come her way to interest and enliven her. The hot, humid dreariness of the season did not help, though the air conditioning, once fully installed, did. She had long since abandoned her habit of sleeping in the study which was now a serious work place and, in her first teaching year, had moved all her clothes and personal things into the guest room which was now her bedroom. Here, soothed by the gentle swish of the new cooler and less conscious of an empty space beside her, she had mainly peaceful nights which made it easier to cope with trying days. She began to feel better. Then she had to deal with an unexpected disappointment. Hari told her that their congenial dinners would have to stop for a while because he was going to Delhi to set up a branch of his business there, leaving his Bombay office in the temporary charge of a brother-in-law. He was leaving at the beginning of October and expected to be away for about three months. She tried not to think about how much she would miss him.

EIGHTEEN

Towards the end of December, Ann herself was back in Delhi for what was becoming her habitual Christmas visit. She found Freni waiting with some hard questions.

"I've had a phone call from your friend, Harilal Chand. He wants to see you while you are here and considered it polite to speak to me about it. How good a friend is he exactly?"

"I've told you. A very good friend. I've always liked him and found him interesting. We enjoy talking to each other."

"Ann! I have in fact met him. Rustam was introduced to him by some business contacts and is somehow involved in a new venture of his, so we had him here for dinner. I admit that I was curious and wanted to look him over. When he came into the house, I thought to myself, 'He's no Adonis', but then he smiled at me and I have to say that my knees went weak. He is a very attractive and impressive man. Where is all this leading?"

"I'm not sure. I'll be honest. I know about the weak knees. I've had some unsettling moments thinking about how I might once have upset Sam when we all used to meet. I did flirt with Hari but it was always very light-hearted. He has never said anything but he probably has some feelings for me. I admit that I'm afraid of myself. I don't want to stop meeting him but I can't think beyond that. I can't bear the idea of putting anyone in Sam's place."

"My dearest girl, be realistic! As I've said before, you are still young. You are going to have natural needs. I have to be brutal. Sam is dead. You can't kill off everything alive in yourself to compensate for that. And don't be devious. Of course Hari still has feelings for you. He hasn't been seeing you all this time just because he enjoys your conversation. You need to admit that and think sensibly about the future. Rustam tells me that, as a businessman, Hari plays a long game but when he sees the right moment, he acts fast and I think he is playing a waiting game with you. I've made my plans too. I have already invited him here for drinks tomorrow evening and suggested that he should take you on for dinner afterwards. You really need to talk openly to him."

After nearly five years of living alone, Ann was unused to being told what to do but she always forgave Freni for anything she did and rang Hari to say that she was pleased that he would be spending time with these very special friends and that she was looking forward to their proposed outing.

The next evening, as they were leaving after a pleasant, convivial hour, Freni said, "Don't worry about coming back late, Ann. The watchman will let you in. Have a good time. Take care of her Hari."

He looked fully at her. "That's exactly what I intend to do."

They had an excellent meal. Nothing seemed to have changed. Hari knew so much about Ann's days that they talked mainly about his affairs, his new branch, how it was developing and what it was like to live in Delhi.

"I'm not sure where you do live while you are here," Ann said with a note of surprise. "You've never actually told me. Are you staying in a hotel?"

"Good God, no! I've rented a flat but luckily I don't have the bother of servants. The landlord provides a morning cleaning service and I get by with that. I eat out most of the time. I'm very comfortable there. Why don't you come back for a coffee and see it for yourself?"

Ann looked nervous and did not answer.

He leaned towards her and said, with a steelier note in his voice than she had ever heard, "Ann, I've been very patient but this has gone on long enough. I haven't said anything before because I know what you have been through. You were subjected to a terrible ordeal. I knew that it would take a long time for a wound like that to heal. It *has* been a long time. I was willing to wait but I can't go on any longer in the role of faithful friend. Parting from you and being away from you just as we were becoming closer has made that clear to me. Don't pretend that you are unaware of how I really feel. I don't think that what you feel for me is mere friendship either. I understand your fears and hesitations but you wouldn't have been seeing me and sharing these meals with me all this time if you weren't half prepared for what I'm now asking of you."

Ann's voice was shaky, "I don't...... I can't......."

He burst in on her, "I think you can. You have shown how incredibly courageous you can be. I admire you for staying on in India alone. Not only have you carried on with your life, you have refashioned it and found a meaningful job for yourself. You are doing well, but you aren't happy. I think that I could change that. You are no coward. Come back with me and we will see just how brave you are."

Ann couldn't speak but she nodded. Her face was flushed. She felt feverish and breathless and when they stood up to leave her legs almost gave way.

At his flat, he took her coat and coming back to her, held out his arms. With a shuddering sigh, she leant against him and put her head on his shoulder. They stood motionless for some minutes. All Ann's constant, taut control dissolved. She knew now just how spent she was beneath that carapace. She was flooded with a total languor and her body felt soft and light. Then Hari bent and kissed her and at the touch of his lips every part of her exploded out of this dreamy state.

Without speaking, he led her into the bedroom and slowly helped her to undress. He lifted her and put her down on the bed and she lay there her eyes closed, hardly breathing, until she felt his weight beside her and turned to him with a small cry. He was delicate in everything he did but it was not in any way an uncertain or passionless delicacy. Ann responded to his slow gentleness with a surprising violence that moved him to urgency and at last they lay side by side for several sleepy moments. Ann looked at Hari. His eyes were closed. She got up, gathered her clothes and went into the adjoining bathroom.

She was there a long time. Hari, pulling on his clothes, went over to the door.

"Are you alright Ann?"

She came out and, to his alarm and dismay, he saw that she was weeping.

"Don't. Don't. I can't bear to see you upset." He tried to take her in his arms but she moved away from him. "What is it Ann? Don't feel that this has been a sign of my not taking you seriously. I intend to behave honourably. I want to marry you."

This provoked a renewed burst of tears.

"It's not very good for my ego to see you like this," Hari tried for a lighter note.

"You don't have to have any fears on that score, Hari." Ann attempted an equally light response but her voice trembled. "I know that I'm being impossible. I'm sorry. I feel so bad. I shouldn't say this to you but…….." She was unable to go on.

"You had better be quite frank. My hope is that we are going to share a life. You should be able to share your thoughts with me."

"My thoughts will hurt you."

"You may or may not have realised from what has just passed between us, but I am not an inexperienced boy. Of course I haven't been close to another person in the way that you already have but I know well enough that loving someone will inevitably mean being hurt from time to time and that accepting the hurt proves the love."

"Oh Hari, I've been alone so long. I've craved to be touched and loved. What has just happened was wonderful." She reached out and taking his hand, held it against her cheek. "I don't want to be like this but I simply can't stop myself thinking of Sam. I know what you will say. Freni says it to me all the time." She moved her shoulders as if gathering strength. "Sam is gone. After all this time I should let him go. But I still need him to have had that unique thing in his life – the way we felt about each other. I thought I could take love without giving it again but you have changed things and I'm shaken by what's happening. You'll think I am crazy, but I have such a vivid picture of Sam, alone and bereft of all the things that he has lost and I feel so treacherous."

"How can I think you are crazy? I think you are loyal, loving, wonderful, and that you have a special way of looking at the world. I can see why I love you. Do you remember our conversation about love so long ago? My words, my facile cleverness, have come back to bite me. I now know how real love is. It isn't only that I want you in the way that I have just made clear – I want to share all that goes on in your mind. Ann, we would be so good for each other. I don't ask you to forget Sam but you can't spend the rest of your life on your own. That is more than he would ask of you. Please. Marry me."

"I can't Hari. I can't tell you, I don't have to tell you, what you have done for me tonight. I wanted you. I wanted to be happy again and believed that I could be happy with you, but I'm suddenly afraid. It isn't just guilt over Sam. I can't do this all over again. It wasn't easy to change my life in the way that I did for him or to deal with the consequences of choosing to change and I've made terrible mistakes. No-one has ever really known just how much to blame I was for what happened to Sam. You say that I was brave to carry on here but that wasn't bravery. I just felt that there was nothing else to do and that I owed it to him to do it. You know that I would have to change again to live with you. What if, in the end, I let you down in the same way? I can't take any more risks. I can't marry you."

Hari took her in his arms and this time she didn't resist him but rested her head wearily on his chest. He stroked her hair.

"You aren't thinking clearly, Ann. We've been through a very emotional experience. Don't torment yourself. You can't make any decisions right now. I won't press you. I shouldn't have rushed you like this. I'll take you back to Freni's. I've been a fool and timed this badly in every way. I can't see you tomorrow. I've arranged a visit to a factory some distance from Delhi that I can't postpone and I shall be staying there with the manager overnight. I'll call you the day after tomorrow. That will give you time to think things over. Don't panic. I do understand how it is for you but I am absolutely sure that we could have a wonderful life together."

He drove her back and held her close for a moment, then gave her a quick kiss on the cheek as he said goodnight.

When she came down to breakfast the next day, Freni said, "You came back very late. Have you talked to Hari?"

"He wants to marry me," Ann said. "I've been awake and thinking about him all night. I wanted his companionship, his attention and yes, what we never speak of but both understand that I need, but I can't marry him. My feelings for him are much stronger than I realised and I can't cope with them. I've made a decision that will shock and hurt you, Freni. I'm going home. I don't mean to Bombay. I mean to England. I'm going to cut all my ties with India. I can't see Hari again but I can't imagine being here without seeing him. It's all too much for me. When I met Sam, I rushed headlong away from all that I was taught to be and thought that I could become part of his world. Sam tried to make that less difficult for me by cutting himself off from so much but it ended in disaster. I can't go through all that again. It has to stop. Last night, I suddenly thought, 'Hari is a Hindu!' That sounds mad. Of course I've always known that he is but he's so sophisticated, so cosmopolitan that I tend to forget. I suddenly realised that, essentially, he belongs to yet another world, one that I would find far more complex and alien than the one I shared with Sam. You know that. I remembered Hari telling me about his mother and sisters. He once told me how they didn't want him to marry after his father died. His mother still plays a big part in his life. There's a female guard around him to whom I'll once more be an outsider, an invader. They won't willingly accept me and take me in. I have to go home. People there think that I've been a fool but they know me and I'm one of them whatever I've done. I'll be where I belong. Oh Freni! You have been so good to me. I'm behaving abominably but I'm suddenly so tired. I just want a quiet life. England is where I'll find that."

"You aren't thinking straight. You're talking nonsense." Freni had looked increasingly horrified as this outpouring went on. "What are you doing now but again rushing headlong into something? Something that you will certainly come to regret! The emotional repression, the parochial attitudes that you once ran away from, do far more harm than being open to change, open to feeling. What sort of life is it, if you can't be happy for fear of being made unhappy? Why live at all? And how can you even imply that we haven't taken you in? You know how dear you are to me."

"I'm sorry. I'm so sorry." Ann's voice shook.

Freni tried to reason with her, to make her see how much she would lose in rejecting Hari, in rejecting them all. Like Clifford and Edna before her, she came up against the unexpected obstinacy that had defeated them. Ann, tearful but determined, insisted on getting her things together and leaving for Bombay early the next day.

"I never thought I'd see you acting like this." Freni was furious. "Never mind what you are doing to us. This is not the way to treat someone who loves you. You can't leave without meeting Hari. He deserves better of you."

"I know what he deserves. I can't give it. I daren't meet him. I have to go."

When Hari rang, Freni broke the news that Ann had already left for Bombay and told him what had passed between them.

"Can't you talk to her, Freni? She is very close to you. She relies on you so. Can't you persuade her to change her mind?"

Freni's voice was sad, "We all think of her as composed, sensible, but beneath that very English facade there is a volcanic centre, Hari. I think that right now she is driven by her fear of that volcano inside her. She thinks that she is running away from you, from India, but she is trying to run away from herself. She's told me quite a bit about her early life. She was programmed to mistrust strong emotions. She thought she had overcome that conditioning and could live fearlessly and freely but I can see she is afraid that she hasn't the energy, given how badly it turned out, to be so bold a second time. Let her go. I think, I hope, that it won't take long for her to realise what a huge mistake she is making, that she will come back to us."

"It will be too late," Hari sounded grim. "I have waited so long already and I can't believe that she has just gone off like this without a word. She has totally ignored my feelings. Of course my instinct is to go after her but I may have to be dramatic too. I may also resort to self-preservation. I hope that she does come back to you. You have done so much for her. It must break *your* heart to be cast aside this way."

Freni sighed. "Luckily I am battle hardened. I have had a fortunate life but I am old enough to have learned to deal with most things that are thrown at me. It is much worse for you. If you feel able, keep in touch. I shall quite understand if you'd prefer not to."

Ann had left Delhi in a blind rush, as if it were possible to leap untrammelled from one existence to another, but it took time to dismantle her Bombay life. She had to give a month's notice at the college and had a difficult interview with Sister Frances who, though calling on all her Christian charity, was visibly put out by this abrupt desertion after all her efforts on Ann's behalf. She could understand her desire to return to England but not the unexplained haste of her departure. Zal and Perin professed sadness at her news but Ann no longer believed that they would be genuinely sorry to see her go. Their treatment of her, while publicly dutiful, had become increasingly perfunctory. They were trying, and to Ann's jaundiced eye managing, to put Sam out of their minds. All their attention centred on Cyrus, who now had a baby girl. Perin had her longed for grandchild. Recalling the bitter night that had followed Cyrus's wedding and her thoughts about the children she and Sam might have had, her failure to find a true place in his family that could survive his death, hardened Ann's resolve and strengthened her determination to go.

She was lacerated by thoughts of what she had done to Hari. Being rejected so brutally after the tenderness of their physical closeness must have been particularly humiliating. In a secret part of her mind she had an image of him as a strong, irresistible force that could sweep her along, free of all her inconsistencies. Was she hoping that this is how he would act? Was she testing him? Testing herself? She knew that she had no clear-cut motivation. She was a welter of conflicting feelings.

Whatever had driven her, she had ended it. There was no word from him. She had no way back. This was very plain when she finally did get a letter from him shortly before she was due to leave India.

Bombay
16/3/76

Ann,

I find it difficult to bring myself to write to you. You have hurt me very badly. The way you went off without a word, thought, or even written communication, was worse than cruel – it seemed contemptuous. I tried very hard to understand the forces that drove you to behave so callously. I have spent some very painful hours since you left me, torn this way and that. My first instinct was to come after you, to plead with you, but in the end I decided, like you, to opt for safety. How could I trust you with my life? You will remember my once telling you about our practical Hindu marriages. Well, my mother will arrange one for me. I shall settle for a simple, orthodox wife who will make me comfortable. I try not to think how I could have had so much more. I hope that you find the peace you claim to be looking for, so that this will have all been worthwhile.

Hari.

His letter was a thunderbolt. It ripped through her and plunged her into abject misery but she was too bruised for tears and her extreme emotion only confirmed her belief that, if she had acted badly, she had acted rightly. She had looked to Hari for consolation, an end to loneliness but had

210

ignited a passion that threatened to overshadow what she'd had with Sam. If she gave in to it she would never escape a taint of faithlessness and she was too exhausted to put herself through further agonies of conscience. On a rational level, Hari's intention to ask his mother to arrange a marriage for him confirmed her fear of the strength and potential dangers of his orthodox hinterland and allowed her to convince herself that she had behaved sensibly.

She determinedly re-focussed her thoughts on Sam. At the end of another sleepless night, she went into their old bedroom which had long been neat and pristine in readiness for her rare visitors.

"That's my marriage," she thought, "unused, sterile." She knelt beside what had been their shared bed and put her head down on Sam's side of it.

"I've really tried Sam," she whispered, "I loved you so much. I wanted to hold on to you and what we had here but I'm so lonely. I can't go on but I can't bear to try again with someone else. I can only survive if I go back to where I started. Do you remember how I spoke once of all that my father would never share with us? I thought that was hard to bear. If I let myself think of all that you won't share with me, it is unendurable. I have to try to forget. I have to go. This time I really *am* leaving you."

She ached with a cold misery that froze tears but she shook herself out of this. "What am I doing? I'm talking to an empty space. The truth is that I am talking to myself. I don't know what I want and this isn't helping. I'll just go home and hope that there I'll find some way to be happy again."

Zal, though emotionally inept, was unequalled in dealing with business matters. He now saw it as his natural role to help her by selling the flat after she left and settling her financial affairs. There were restrictions on taking money out of India but, through reciprocal arrangements with connections of his, he could overcome these difficulties and ensure the transfer of a considerable sum to her account in England. He immediately fulfilled one of her most urgent requirements in setting up a fund that would provide Kishen with a life pension.

Telling Kishen that she was leaving was heart-rending.

"I shall miss you so much. You have been such a help to me all this time. I hate to leave you and take away your work, your place here, but I have to go home."

She explained what she had done to secure an income for him for the rest of his life. "This means that you too can go home if you want to and be with your family. Of course if you would rather continue working in Bombay, I will find a good position for you."

"No, Memsahib, I cannot work for other person if I am not to work for you." Kishen's normally imperturbable face was creased with the effort of maintaining control. "I will go to my village and work on our land. But Ram is young. He will not like to go back. He will want to stay in city."

His nephew had also been faithful all these years and Ann promised that he would be found a suitable job. Kishen was relieved and bowed his head. The nature of the bond between them was such that, though they had always been conscious of their respect and affection for each other, this had never been demonstrated in any way. They had maintained strict boundaries.

Now Ann could not stop herself from taking both his hands.

"Oh Kishen! You have always made a sad and dreadful time more bearable for me. I will truly grieve not to see you each day, so cheerful, so kind, and so helpful."

They were both holding back tears. Kishen stepped back, folded his hands in the traditional gesture and again bowed his head.

"I have been a lucky man to have served you, Memsahib. I thank you for taking care of me still, even when you will be far away. I will never forget you and Sahib. There has been a great sadness here. I pray that you will find happiness back in your home with your people."

Two months later, as Ann walked away from a small group of family and friends, to find her place on what she expected to be her last flight from this crowded, heaving airport with its many associations, it was this that she remembered as the most moving of all the farewell speeches that she had heard.

NINETEEN

This time there was no one waiting for her when she landed at Heathrow. She was not going on directly to Norfolk. She had acted so precipitately that she had nowhere to go there. The current tenancy on the cottage still had some weeks to run and, painfully aware that her return could be viewed as a defeat, the idea of staying with her grandparents on those terms was too much for her. She had arranged for a cleaner to go in and prepare the place for her after the present occupants moved out and had booked into a hotel for a month.

Even after her years in Bombay she was not a natural city-dweller but she was accustomed to navigating the complexities of a large urban sprawl and London did not frighten her. For all her intense, impetuous behaviour, she was capable of hard-headedness and she looked on her weeks here as a reconnaissance mission. She might well want to come back from time to time in the years ahead if village life became claustrophobic.

She finally arrived home, unannounced, in a hired car, on a bright, windy afternoon in mid-April. She stood in the rather unkempt front garden, with her face upturned to the huge sky that had overarched her childhood, and took several deep breaths before opening the heavy, wooden door and stepping into the dark, panelled hallway where she was met by a remembered scent of mingled leather and lavender. Tentatively, and trembling a little, she went into each room. Anything remotely personal – books, pictures, ornaments – had long ago been crated up by her cousin as she had requested and she intended this to be a business-like exploration of the state of her property rather than a pilgrimage, but the faded, old-fashioned wallpapers, which had never been changed, caught at her heart.

It did not take long to install herself in her old bedroom. She had only her immediate clothes and toiletries to unpack and put away. Charles had promised to send over the stored boxes later and her Bombay possessions were coming by sea. They were very few. She had ruthlessly discarded almost everything other than her clothes and personal things, keeping only her books and teaching materials – the concrete, un-shadowed components of the one positive outcome of all her years away – though, at the very last minute, she had packed up some of the things that she and Sam had most cherished and asked Zal and Perin to keep them. She had no idea why she had done so. Did she ever mean to reclaim them? She could not imagine bringing them here.

Although her grandparents had known that she was coming that day, she had not told them exactly when, feeling the need to face the cottage on her own, but her grandmother had insisted that, for her first few days, she should have her supper with them. So, early that evening, she walked the short distance across the fields to their farm. The blustery wind had now died down but there was still a light breeze blowing and it was a joy to walk briskly again without discomfort, her body light and dry. Once or twice she stopped to take in the spacious emptiness around her and the almost total quiet, broken only by the sound of moving air and occasional birdsong.

When she reached the farmhouse, a stately building fronting a small stream, she by-passed the main door, which was rarely opened, and went round to the yard gate. As she lifted the latch, a farmworker wheeled his bicycle out of a barn, ready to set off for home.

"Tom!" her voice rose.

She had known this man since she was a girl. He was a little more weather-beaten and bent but not greatly changed. He came up to her.

"That's good to see you home, Ann." He nodded towards the house. "They'll be pleased to have you back."

He stood beside her for a few moments without speaking but perfectly at ease, and then mounted his bike.

"Ah well, I'll be off. My tea will be getting cold." He rode away without another look.

"He's been going home at exactly this time every evening, all the years that I've been gone," she thought. She was smiling as she went on into the house. That was how it was going to be. No fuss. No flag waving.

That was how it was. Her grandparents, also little changed, did ask her about the cottage and her plans for it and then the conversation flowed in the usual channels – local affairs, the weather prospects and the current jobs on the farm. If she had once found taking up her Bombay habits like floating out into a warm pool, this was like wading into a cool river.

In her first few days, she woke dazed and disorientated. Where was Kishen with her morning tea? She quickly became accustomed to catering for herself and, like her mother, had a weekly cleaner. It was not Kishen's practical help but his unemphatic, reliable presence in the background of all she did that she missed and she allowed herself to miss him for a while as a tribute to his years of quiet loyalty. She had indulged in wild plans to totally eradicate India from her life but, like a haunting tune, well known but momentarily just beyond grasp, it was embedded in her subconscious and a vivid image, woven of heat, dust, spicy aromas, plaintive music, vibrant colours and the non-stop noise and movement of irrepressibly curious, lively, undaunted people, would sometimes leap into her mind and pierce her with a sense of loss. However illogical it was, she often felt homesick for a place she had rejected, a place where she no longer wished to be.

She did struggle to forget. She firmly smothered any tendency to dwell on her wistful sense of Sam's absence. She had been wrong never to bring him here, to a place and to people that were so much part of her. She believed that he had understood that she wasn't ashamed of him, that he had recognised her ingrained dread of discomfort and embarrassment, but she was troubled to find herself undeservedly benefitting from this dereliction. To everyone here, Sam was shadowy, almost fictional. They had not seen him, talked to him or shared any part of their lives with him. He had no place in their mental landscape or their conversations. There were no reminders. She had only her own thoughts of him to suppress.

All her recollections of Hari were savagely excised but she had, against all reason, half expected that Freni would persist with her and would write, telephone or even visit. She did not see her as someone to give up easily. There was not a word. She had not only disappointed this dearest of friends, she had infuriated her. Freni had been greatly impressed with Hari, seen him as perfect for Ann and considered her treatment of him as cowardly and heartless. She almost certainly felt her own treatment to have been equally shabby. It seemed that she could not forgive this. Ann knew that she was being unfair but the rebuff stung her. She still received letters from Perin whose sense of family duty was strong and who possibly still regretted her own part in all that had happened, but her replies were mired in the same difficulty that she had once found in writing to Edna. There was so much that had to be explained, so much that was alien to her mother-in-law and these exchanges slowly dwindled to rare updates and formal expressions of goodwill. The past was receding. A door was closing.

It took her six months to renovate and re-colonise the cottage. She did not alter it greatly, merely refreshed it. As the days passed, it became increasingly inviting and restful and she began to find something of the peace she so much wished for. It could occasionally be a mournful place, but if her parents haunted it in any way, there was such a long history of good times with them imprinted on its walls that any such sadness could be overcome. It was wonderful not to get up each day to noisy mayhem or to step outside into humidity and heat. She delighted in the silence and the invigorating air that she had once taken for granted. Yet there were long, blank periods when she sorely regretted the loss of her students, her friends and the challenges of an ever-changing, if exhausting, city existence.

She filled such empty hours by starting on the garden, which was very overgrown and uncared for. Her grandfather sent over two men to help with the really heavy digging and clearing and wanted them to do even more than that.

"Those tenants of yours have let it get into a right old state. That's too much for you to handle. I don't want you to injure yourself, girl."

But Ann insisted on doing most of the work herself, finding that days of hard physical labour ensured that she slept well and was not troubled by wakeful nights, filled with unsettling memories. Slowly, though, what she first used as an exercise yard to grind herself into a state of utter exhaustion that carried her beyond the reach of sorrow and sleeplessness became a creative and fulfilling source of pleasure. On fine mornings she started to take her morning tea outside and would sit watching the birds that she had encouraged in with feeders and bird baths. This bustle of intense life gave a cheering start to her day and, after the silence of her solitary bedroom, was a heart-lifting delight. She regularly walked around her large plot both to enjoy what had already been completed and to plan future planting. On these walks, she would often be transfixed by sudden glimpses of perfection; small miniature paintings, framed pictures that she had created with colour, texture and contrast. It was intensely satisfying. She began to see her garden, like her teaching in Bombay, as one of the positive things that she had achieved – something to offset all her mistakes and misjudgements.

Once the cottage, the garden and her household arrangements were settled, she was overtaken by a characteristic restlessness. Walking down the local High Street and passing what had been her father's shop, she could not help wondering if she might have been happier if she had stayed and lived the life that he had planned for her. After his death, his stock had been bought by a friend in the trade and the empty premises sold. It was now a dress shop. It was a reminder of lost contentment and her father's lost dreams but she could not honestly feel it as a lost opportunity. Ironically, it had been part of her father's plan that she should spend time in Cambridge and, therefore, his doing that she had met Sam, gazed into his eyes and recklessly discarded all the staid prohibitions of this small town by walking into the night with a stranger. This was an apt metaphor. She had paid a heavy price for her rashness and had walked into a far darker and more sorrowful life than she could ever have imagined, but had also walked into a wider, more exciting world. If she had lost love, she had at least known a far more intense form of it than anything she would ever have found here. She had to reconcile herself to loss and, back where she had started, find another way to live.

She missed her teaching. It was something she was extremely good at. She enjoyed the contact with students and the thrill of firing them with her own enthusiasms but in England everything had its rules and regulations and she could not take it up in the casual way that had been possible in Bombay. She had learned from her time away, however, that a way round problems could usually be found and searching the area discovered a private language school in Norwich that had recently been set up by a forty year old Cambridge graduate. After seeing all the certificates that she had acquired in India and receiving testimonials from Sister Frances, who was still heroically willing to help her out, he was happy to take her on as a teacher. He did, though, ask her to take a short, part time course in teaching English as a foreign language run by the Royal Society of Arts.

"I'm taking something of a financial risk in starting up this school, Mrs Mehta. There are many such places opening just now and, unfortunately, some of them are less professional than they might be. To be really successful, mine must be seen as a reputable, first class institution. Your qualifications are more than adequate, and your experience of living and teaching within a foreign environment invaluable, but a recognised, English certificate would help and it will be something that you can easily acquire."

Anxious to be as busy as possible and grateful for the chance to teach again, Ann was happy to enrol in the recommended course. She bought herself a small car and drove up to Norwich every weekday, sometimes staying overnight to go to the theatre or a concert. She regained a working week and something of a cultural life.

She even began accepting invitations for a pub lunch or an evening meal from her new employer. Like her, he came from a local, rural community. In graduating and going on to set up a business, he had moved beyond this background, but not so far beyond it as to seem alarmingly exciting, and he had the familiar, stolid calm of her relatives. She felt a qualm at this cold blooded assessment but she did like him and as he showed no sign of any stronger feelings towards her than an appreciation of their shared interests, and an obvious wish to use her skills – including her almost forgotten secretarial training – to improve and expand the school, she felt fairly safe with him.

Her mother's parents had always been hospitable in an unostentatious way. Her grandmother, a talented cook, enjoyed preparing substantial meals and their farm had always been very much the hub of family life. Although it had hit them hard and they were never quite as active as before, the tranquil flow of their lives had closed over Edna's death and they still liked to gather people around them for a Sunday lunch or a special holiday. Her Uncle James completely managed her paternal grandfather's farm and entertained only very occasionally, but Ann was frequently in the company of relatives and old friends at both farmhouses.

She often found herself the youngest person present. Many of her contemporaries were now dispersed around the country, finding new jobs in towns and cities and marrying outsiders. The old, tight closeness of this rural community was loosening. Younger cousins and friends who were tied to farms stayed on, but changing methods of working the land were also changing them. Even here things moved more swiftly. Attitudes were more open. People were more likely to travel. Holidays abroad were becoming common. Yet, there was still a degree of disinterest in a wider world. Ann with many reasons for reticence was, nevertheless, sometimes betrayed into comments on her experiences in India. She found that any such remarks fell into an unresponsive blankness and another subject would be quickly raised. It was quite likely that their knowledge of all that had happened to her there and an embarrassed concern for her feelings might deter those who knew her from following up on what she said, but the new people she was meeting behaved in much the same way. She reminded herself that she was actively putting her past behind her and was once again being completely illogical. She did not want to think about India. It was her aim to forget.

By the beginning of her fourth year in England she was, if not exactly fulfilled, reasonably positive. She no longer expected anyone or anything to give her everything she needed but this place and her work gave her what she wanted most, security and freedom from difficult choices. There were times when she was haunted by both Sam and Hari and racked by the longings that thoughts of them stirred in her. There was no-one among her old friends or new colleagues and acquaintances who would ever come near to replacing Jess or Freni. It was undeniably a lonely life but, equally, it was in no way threatening or unpredictable. She had been through so much that this almost frozen neutrality was a relief.

Just as she was learning to live on these terms, she received an unexpected letter from Jess that threw her into disarray. All the misery over their lost friendship, the horror of its ending, flooded back. All the frailties, shortcomings and heart-burning of her time in Bombay were revisited. All that she had fought so long to delete from her consciousness was reinstated by this one piece of paper. But, shaken as she was, the reckless element of her nature took over once more and she sent a reply, inviting Jess to stay for two days. She had no real faith in the possibility of reconciliation but she felt a need to confront both her old friend and all her own uncertainties, to put to rest any doubts she still had about what had happened all that time ago. She also needed to finally convince herself that she had done the right thing and was in the right place, that nothing could undermine her resettlement in her old home, her resumption of her old ways.

TWENTY

"What happened that night? That morning?" The question hung over them like a sudden small cloud chilling and darkening the sunny peace of the garden. Jess moved her head restlessly as if trying to shake this off.

"Ann, there's something that I haven't told you. I didn't put it in my letter. I was afraid of how you would take it. I'm going to Bombay next month."

"You can't!"

"I can. It's all fixed. You must remember Sarla Patel and how friendly I was with her. Well, she and I have kept in touch all this time and she always says that she misses me. When I told her that I was in England for some time, without Bob, she asked me to go for a short visit."

Jess hesitated but, with a sideways glance at Ann, added rather aggressively, "She said that the past was the past and she only lives in the present."

"It's madness." Ann's voice was strong but she knew this to be description rather than deterrence.

"No. It isn't mad. I need to go back." Jess was subdued but serious. "I need to face everyone. To end a nightmare."

Ann could hardly believe this shameless assumption of suffering, of victimhood. She had to control an urge to lash out physically but after a long, uncomfortable pause, she shifted in her seat as if easing stiffness or pain and her voice was icily calm as she said, "What does Bob think about your going?"

"He didn't want me to go. He worried about what people would think, how they might behave towards me. Sarla persuaded him that there wouldn't be any problems after so long."

"No problems! That's just too…." Ann stopped short, her teeth clenched with the effort of holding back further angry words. She was determined to see this through, to whatever end, with some degree of dignity. She spoke again slowly and carefully, "I've missed Bob. I have heard nothing from him and had no news of him all this time."

Jess was on the verge of tears. Apparently forgetting what was happening to them, that they were locked in a kind of battle, she fell into a remembered, confidential openness.

"I hurt him very badly and I made things difficult for him in his work. He loved India and because of me he had to leave it. We've been in Beirut and Indonesia and now he's on a temporary posting to Yemen. He thought it best for me not to go there as the conditions would be somewhat harsh and he would only be there for about three months. That's why I'm here in England. We are going to Pakistan next. Bob may possibly get the chance to go back to India in the future but it won't be the same for him as it used to be. He tries hard and he is very good to me but he doesn't feel the same about me either."

Ann made no comment but stared sadly out across the terrace without really seeing anything.

"I'm *so* looking forward to staying with Sarla." For the first time in this disquieting conversation, something of the old Jess surfaced. "She was always such tremendous fun and *so* clever and interesting. She never dropped me and keeps me in touch with what the old crowd are doing." A querulous note entered her voice. "Whatever she says, I don't really know how it will be with them. They all cut me off completely."

"They didn't cut you off. You simply weren't there. Bob had come to the rescue as usual, got you out of things, out of trouble, and you are still trying to avoid trouble." Ann brought them back to reality. "You are simply refusing to answer my question."

Jess leaned across the table, her tone urgent, "Ann, this is hard. We were *so* close you and I. We did everything together. We made life so much better for each other. We were totally honest with each other. We told each other everything. But we were *all* close. Bob was extremely fond of you......and of Sam. It was......"

Ann cut in, "Do you need to tell me? How we were? That's what made it all more unbearable. Don't hedge, Jess. Answer me. What happened that night?"

Jess sat back and looked out over the garden. "Bob and I had noticed for some time that Sam wasn't happy. You more or less told me so yourself. Then you went to Delhi and he was alone. Bob went to Delhi and I was alone. We were both facing a blank, lonely weekend. I thought that if we went out to Mahu together, Sam would feel better."

Ann's voice was fierce and grating, "What happened? As you just said, we were always honest with each other. You were never afraid to say anything you wanted to say. You have to tell me. You can't keep skating around. I'm sure that you are on very thin ice."

Jess turned sharply towards her and said with a shrill note of desperation, "Alright! Alright! You want me to tell you, I'll tell you. You shouldn't have to hear this but you insist on hearing it. I don't want to tell you, but I'll tell you! I'll tell you! Sam and I…. We…." She gave Ann a scared but defiant look, "We made love."

She was unable to hold Ann's gaze but, as if driven to speak now that she had at last broken her long silence, rushed into words again, her face averted and her hands tightly clasped.

"I don't know how it happened. Sam couldn't sleep. He was so restless and sad. I felt so sorry for him. I wanted to comfort him. Suddenly there we were. It just…. happened. Sam was horrified at what we'd done. He was furious with me. He was totally unfair and unreasonable. He turned on me viciously and said really cruel things to me. He was completely changed, cold and harsh. It was three o'clock in the morning but he insisted that we had to go home. He drove like a madman. A car came out in front of us. We swerved. I can't remember what actually happened next. It's a blur of noise and pain." She added shakily, "If I behaved badly, I was soon made to pay. Seeing Sam….so beautiful…so dear……I knew that he was badly hurt. I was hurt too. Then they told me that he was ……." She could not continue. Her shoulders hunched, she was crying soundlessly.

Ann folded her arms around her chest as she had done when first told of Sam's death. She wanted to scream and shout but she forced herself to stay quiet and still. She had, of course, known. Bob had not spelled it out but it had been obvious that something serious had taken place between Sam and Jess. Yet, all these years, she had almost made herself believe that she was reading too much into what he had said, almost persuaded herself that if what had happened was bad, it wasn't the worst, the unforgiveable thing. The stark truth coming at her in blunt words was almost unbearably bitter and wounding.

Jess, even in these straits, could still sound plaintive. "It was partly my fault. I know that. But I didn't intend anything like that when we set out. I only wanted Sam to enjoy Mahu with me. It was such a wonderful place for us all. It was where we spent all our best times. It was one of your favourite places, Ann. You always……"

Ann said savagely, "Can't you see how that makes what you did even more unforgiveable? Partly your fault? You didn't intend? You killed Sam!"

Jess, her face red and puckered, fluttered her hands, fending off this biting accusation, but Ann was cold and insistent, "You killed Sam. You destroyed my life. Yet here you are, still quite ready to make use of, and trample over, all those shared memories."

Jess stopped crying and an overtone of anger hardened her still girlish voice. "Don't forget that you had made Sam extremely miserable. The fact that this was plain to us when he was usually so contained and controlled meant that things were very bad with him. You know that you had treated him shabbily for so long in not taking him to England or allowing him to get to know your family and you admitted to me that you had been punishing him for the death of your father. You went off, leaving him behind. You wrote letters telling him what a good time you were having without him. We were both hurt that you seemed to have forgotten how important you were to us. You made it clear that you had new friends and were managing quite well without us. That night, when I saw him, unable to sleep, lost and forlorn, I wanted to hold him, to make him feel better. It went too far and Sam reacted so extremely, so violently. He was like a stranger. It shouldn't have ended as it did. It will always haunt me. Over and over and over again, I see him lying there."

She broke into sobs. Ann's stomach lurched. While she had been far away, unaware of Sam's last desperate moments, Jess had been with him. She felt faint and dizzy with the horror that the thought of this further intimacy aroused in her and bent her head, blind to everything around her. She held down a primitive urge to hit Jess, to batter her. It was too late for that. She looked up and stared clinically and critically at her. There were no visible scars from the physical injuries that she had received in the crash, but her looks had been subtly damaged. The glow, the gloss had gone. She had put on weight. For the first time ever, forced to face the consequences of her actions and the realisation that there was no guarantee that she should and would always be happy, Jess no longer saw herself as the girl that everyone loved. They had all lost so much. Ann mourned Sam but she also grieved for Bob and, despite her fury, felt a reluctant pity for Jess.

"You were always careless, Jess. Literally care less. You never stopped to think. Look at how you took me, a complete stranger, to your flat that day we met. If you wanted to do something, you just did it. You felt entitled to do anything you pleased." She paused and then added wearily, "But we can't go on like this. It won't change anything and it is harming us both. It was that confidence of yours that fascinated and charmed me. I loved you. I not only lost Sam, I lost you and Bob and a treasured friendship."

Jess was about to speak and Ann held up her hand, her face quite haggard. "Don't say anything. I'm exhausted. I can only think about how we are going to get through this. We can't undo anything that either of us has done. We have to make an attempt to be civilised and sensible. I don't want to add a further shameful chapter to such a sorry story. Go indoors and wash your face. Use the cloakroom in the hall. Then come back here. I've prepared all this food. Let's try to eat."

Jess looked stunned by this descent to the ordinary but she stood up and went into the house without comment or protest. When she returned, Ann was facing out into the garden and spoke without looking at her. "It seems incredible that it is nine years since all this happened. That's time playing tricks again. When I was young it always flowed along smoothly and evenly, but after I met Sam it changed and began to jerk about and confuse me. Sometimes a day could go on forever while a year would pass before I could blink. Now, somehow, almost without my counting them, all these years have passed, years that I should have spent with Sam." She turned a sombre face to Jess. "We can't ever make up for what happened to him. I tried – unrealistically I now see – to make some amends but nothing can change the fact that he never did all the things he hoped to do, that he should have done." She concentrated on the garden again. "Until now, I've always refused to admit that Sam wasn't blameless. I've always thrust such a thought away. It seemed wrong to let myself think badly of him. But you couldn't have caused such devastation in our lives unless he himself had allowed you to. We were all at fault in different ways."

They fell into another long, fraught wordlessness. Then Ann took up a dish and offered it to Jess. "We still have to eat. Presumably after all this time, we have *both* decided to go on living." Her tone was caustic. Then she relented a little, "Take something. Here we are. However impossible it seems, we have to get through this time together somehow. We can't sit here in a hostile silence. We both need to make an effort."

They helped themselves to food and began to eat slowly, without real appetite. The sunshine, the view of the garden, the birds singing around them and the careful prettiness of the table setting all mocked them and heightened the surreal element of the situation.

Ann made the first stilted attempt at ordinary conversation. "You said that Sarla keeps you in touch with news of our old friends. What does she say about them? How are they? What they are doing these days?"

"They seem to be doing much the same things." Jess spoke listlessly. "Sarla is still editing her magazine. Oh!" Her voice lifted. "She did tell me that Hari Chand had married. Apparently, after years as a gay bachelor, he made a very orthodox marriage. It was a great surprise to them all." Her eyes were limpid and perhaps rather too wide open.

Ann's mouth was pinched and her determined return to her usual manner forgotten. She looked coldly at Jess. What else had Sarla told her?

Jess took a huge, indrawn breath, "Ann, you are trying very hard. You always needed to appear cool and self-contained. We both know that you are, in fact, blazingly angry and I am going to say something that will only infuriate you more – but I have to say it. What about you? You are still young. You've been on your own for nine years. You can't spend the rest of your life this way."

Ann was sure that Jess was making connections, had heard something about her and Hari from Sarla and almost spat out her next words.

"You, above all, should understand that I can't think of anyone after Sam. People do live alone. They have good lives. I've also known three strong women who even though they married, didn't... don't, depend on their men to give them a sense of worth. My mother had a good relationship with my father but they were far apart in all that was deepest in them. I realise, now, that in many ways they lived parallel lives. Perin, as you know, may be controlled by Zal when it comes to her actions, but her inner life is a closed book to him. Then Freni..." she hesitated, "You don't know my friend, Freni, of course. Well, she and her husband like each other and respect each other, but she is the epitome of a free spirit."

Jess did not pursue a topic that clearly held alarming possibilities but, after another daunting pause, seemed impelled to risk further conflict. "Sarla mentions you often. She says that she was always sorry not to have seen more of you while you were working in Bombay. She wonders why you have never been back. She has heard that you haven't been to Delhi either. Why have you cut yourself off like that, Ann? When we were younger, everyone saw you as rational and sensible. I was the giddy, impulsive one. But I know you. You can be worse than impulsive, you can be extreme."

She sat for a moment, her eyes a little frightened and then burst out, "You accused me of killing Sam. Sam was India for you. If you give up on it, cut his world out of your life, cut him out of your life, you are killing him a second time."

Ann gripped the edge of the table. She had used up all the self-control she could muster. Somehow she had dredged up the courage to carry on after the blow that Jess had dealt her and managed to endure being close to her, fighting off the revulsion that threatened to overcome her at the thought of what had happened between her and Sam. She had intended to end this as well as possible, hating the thought of her life being further blackened by any squalid denouement, but all the ferocity that she had kept in check so far, boiled up in her. She had to literally hold herself in. "Now you have gone too far. You have absolutely no right to say anything about how I deal with my memories of Sam. How dare you try to tell me how to live when it's your actions that have changed my life so completely? I shouldn't have accused you of killing him. That *was* extreme. But your thoughtless behaviour cost him his life. Just don't pretend that you were thinking of him. You were simply indulging yourself without a thought for anyone else. I have tried to forgive you for any harm that you have done to me but it was always going to be hard to forgive you for what you did to Sam, and I simply won't endure your interference in my present or my future. This is a closed subject, Jess."

They both pushed away their plates and made no further pretence of eating. Jess was very pale.

"There is nothing to be done, is there? You've been forcing yourself to carry on but you should never have put us through this. You should have been honest about your feelings from the start. You have been sitting here, quiet and dangerous, like an unexploded hand grenade. You may say that you don't hate me but it's obvious that you do. It's impossible for me to stay on. We shall only continue to outrage and wound each other. I'll go back straight away. I was hoping for so much from this, from coming here. I do know how awful it has all been. I do know what harm I did. I just had this crumb of hope that, after so long and after all that we once were to each other, there just might be some way back."

She stood up. Without answering her, Ann went indoors and fetched her suitcase. Bringing it out and setting it down beside her, was answer enough. They walked round to the car together and stood awkwardly beside it. Jess made a move towards Ann, who stepped sharply away from her.

"Ah well." Jess, her lips quivering, got into the car. She leaned out of the window and managed a final flash of bravado, "Luckily I hadn't even unpacked. Enjoy the wine and the chocolates."

TWENTY-ONE

Once Jess had driven off, Ann returned to the terrace and started to gather up the dismal remnants of their half-eaten lunch.

"Another disaster," she thought grimly. "Once again I seem to have made a huge effort only to be left with nothing but a mess to show for it. There's no point in running away from this one though."

She moved slowly, heavily, as she cleared the table and after putting everything away in the kitchen, came back outside and slumped in her chair.

"We made love." These words gnawed at her. Her memories of Sam had always been potently physical and there was no escape from searing thoughts of him and Jess together. Nor, having heard exactly what had happened on that dreadful night, was there any escape from the stark fact of his part in all this. She could take her share of the blame and acknowledge that she had treated him shabbily. She could admit that in refusing to allow him into her family and her home she had been selfish and cowardly and recognise that she had compounded her shoddy behaviour by implicitly reproaching him after her father died. She could understand how her escape to Delhi might well have made him feel lonely and rejected but, whatever excuses she made for him, he had still been guilty and, by being unfaithful with her best friend, guilty of a double betrayal. His uncontrolled reaction to that guilt had led to an avoidable tragedy. When she had re-ordered her life without him, she had wilfully ignored that truth, refused to take it into account, determinedly holding on to her ideal of him. Her showdown with Jess had shattered such complacency. She was shaken by the idea of how horribly this blind obstinacy might have led her astray and caused her to make catastrophic decisions about her future.

After sitting in shocked misery for some considerable time, she roused herself and walked out into the garden but found no relief there, lost in wrenching thoughts of how badly all her closest relationships had ended: her parents and Sam dead; Jess and Bob lost to her; Perin and Zal distant and withdrawn; Hari rejected and in retreat within his marriage; Freni alienated by her behaviour; Kishen used for so long as a prop and then abandoned. Perhaps she deserved to be alone. All she now had were relatives, local acquaintances and a few casual connections among her Norwich colleagues. They were all very much in the background of her existence, rather like the tambura drone in Indian music, soothing, setting the tonic, but heard at some level below consciousness. There was no melody. Friendship having failed her, having in her turn failed friendship, she had made no further serious attempt at it. Love having caused such pain, she had been too frightened to embrace the chance to experience it again. Downgraded and diminished, her life had become this paltry, timid thing with safety and tranquillity her only goals. Brought up to see this as a good way to live, she had once travelled a huge literal and mental distance into a far more demanding and exciting emotional landscape and, reminded of that early passion and commitment, was forced to see just how little she had settled for. She had vowed to make something in her life matter, as a tribute to Sam, but, in truth, she owed this to herself as much as to him. She no longer expected her life to be extraordinary but what she had wasn't enough. She deserved more. She had to find more.

She spent a miserable, restless night, only falling into a brief exhausted sleep just before dawn but the next morning, as always on summer days, she took her morning tea outside and lifting her face to the pleasant breeze, felt her tired, sore eyes soothed and her tension eased. It was a Sunday that was to have been spent with Jess and now she had a whole day ahead of her with nothing planned. She had time to think things through and, hopefully, by the time she went to Norwich on Monday morning she could have put this dreadful encounter behind her and recovered sufficiently to be capable of working as usual.

Already her garden and the sun were regaining some of their magic and she began to revive, to feel a little more hopeful. She decided to have her breakfast on the terrace. She had to obliterate the stain of yesterday's confrontation and erase Jess from this special place. Having her usual pleasant meals here would not be sufficient to do that. She had to deal with the emotions that their frank talk had unleashed and find answers to the questions it had raised.

Jess had hit a nerve in criticising her rejection of India. She must find the courage to admit that she had made a mistake. She would make a determined effort to renew her ties with Zal and Perin. Surely they could find a space for her and bear having her with them after all this time. Their life was now centred on Cyrus and his family and their grief over Sam would have softened. She would write to them, tell them how sorry she was that they had grown so distant from each other and ask if she could visit them.

Jess must be finally forgotten. Could she recover what she had shared with another close friend? If she did go back to India, Freni was the person who could best help her to be at ease there again. It might also be possible somehow to see Kishen again.

Her thoughts were racing and a mood of optimism washed through her. When she had sailed to Bombay in 1965, it had seemed like an epic journey, but nowhere was that far away any more. You would need to go into space to have that old sense of enormous distance. Perspectives and attitudes, too, had changed over the fifteen years since her marriage. It wasn't just a case of her going to India, she could invite old Bombay friends here. That had always seemed impossible but it wasn't such a big thing. The impossibility had always been to some extent a creation of her own fears and worries. She had judged everyone else to be insular but maybe she had been the one that was narrow-minded. Why had she agonised about all that for so long?

She jumped up filled with a restless need for action but then forced herself to sit down again. She must not make any further dramatic gestures. She had to take a balanced view of the people and experiences that mattered to her and find a sensible way to accommodate them all. One thing was clear. Whatever else she decided to do, she must hold on to the life she had here. It might seem simple and unexciting but it was the only solid base that she had to build on. She sat on the edge of her chair for only ten minutes. She fully intended to stay calm, not to be reckless or hasty, but she could not wait. She rushed indoors and grabbing some notepaper and a pen from her desk, took them through into the kitchen, her established comfort zone. She sat at the oak table and began to write.

Long Meadow Cottage
17/5/80

Dear Perin,

I hardly know how to begin this letter. It is so long since we have really said anything important to each other. Still, whatever difficulties we had over the years, we usually tried to be honest with each other and I want to be honest now. I knew how hard it was for everyone when Sam married me but, at that time, I was very young and green and too taken up by my own feelings to think much about other people. I allowed love to blind me to many things and, later, I twice allowed grief to blind me again. I see everything more clearly now and I want to say sorry for all that I have done to lead to us becoming so distant. I have recently been forced to think back to what happened after we lost Sam and been made to realise that I also lost a great deal in giving up everything that I shared with you. You know that I really did try to carry on in Bombay without him and that, for a while, it seemed that I would manage to make a second life there, but I was very lonely and, when I could find no acceptable answer to that loneliness, I suddenly longed to be back in what I then saw as my real home. I was so tired. I think you will understand what drove me at that

point. I am contented here. I miss my parents but it is comforting to be back in our cottage. I am surrounded by family and old friends and I get enormous pleasure from my garden. I have already told you that I am teaching at a language school about forty minutes drive from here. There now seems to be a real possibility that I shall be able to take on a bigger role there with some additional administrative responsibility. I do enjoy my work and it is good to be able to use all the training and experience that I gained in Bombay, to feel that all the effort that I put into it has not been wasted. But I am not just writing to give you all this news. I wanted to tell you that, though I had to come home, I was wrong to try to forget my Indian life. There was no need to be so extreme. I would like to see you all and make a new start. Could I come and visit you? I will shortly begin a long summer holiday and, if you can have me, it should still be possible to make arrangements to come to Bombay then. I hope you think it is sad that things have come to this and would also like us to get back to something of our old, friendlier ways.
With all my love,
Ann.

Talking to Perin had always been unexpectedly easy and she was happy with what she had managed to say. It was more difficult to know what to write in the other letter she wanted to send and twice she made a start, only to crumple the paper impatiently and take a fresh sheet but once she did manage to begin, the words flowed onto the paper.

Long Meadow Cottage
17/5/80

Dear Freni,

I am sitting here in my very English kitchen where I spend so much time trying to be my very English self. Oh, Freni! I have been unutterably stupid and wrongheaded. You are a surgeon's daughter. What sort of ectomy is it when someone tries to cut out a vital part of everything that has made them what they are? I'm no longer the rural Norfolk girl I've been pretending to be all this time since I left you. Of course, after all that I went through, there are consolations in returning to a place that was home for so long, to people who have known me since I was a child, but I've at last been made to realise that, however soothing this is, it isn't enough. How could I have been so foolish as to lose all contact with a friend who had become so important to me and had held me together through the most dreadful experience of my life? Freni, you may have given up on me. I have been ungrateful and callous. I can't believe that I could have cut you off like this for so long. I may have so disgusted you that you feel that you never want to see me again but please try to forgive me. I may not deserve your friendship but I do long to see you. In my heart, I trust you and your generosity. You are not a petty person. Please write to me. I will wait anxiously for your reply. I have written to Zal and Perin to ask if I can come to visit them very soon. I want to come back to India, not to stay, but to bring it back into my life again. It is inescapably in my life. Sam is inescapably part of my life. I know how much you hate platitudes but I think you would agree that, even though it led to pain and grief, I was lucky to share a special love with him. I can't pretend that I have forgotten Hari but it truly wasn't in me to deal with such intense feelings again. I have many regrets but, in that, I couldn't have acted in any other way. If much that might have been, will never be possible for me in India, my best hope is that I can make what does remain there an integral, meaningful part of any future I have. I shall stay in England. I love the cottage and I am getting enormous satisfaction from creating a beautiful garden. I am teaching again at a language school in Norwich and making a reasonable life here, even if at times it is rather lonely. Despite all my fears and my possibly irrational need to be faithful to Sam, I don't want to be so solitary. I never hid things from you and trying to talk to you again, even on paper, has made me admit a thought that I have actually been hiding from myself. I meet several pleasant men in the course of my work and am, in fact, getting more closely involved with the man who employs me. He is asking me to help out on the administrative side of the school he runs. All this makes me see that a marriage like that of my parents, placid, friendly, posing few dangers, may be possible for me one day. It would be a way of ending loneliness but in my mind of keeping faith with my first and special love. For now I need true friends. Home for me is probably no longer a particular place but a way of living easily with both my worlds. You are my dearest and most important link with one of them.

*I really need to see you again and try to find a way back
to the understanding we shared. Please write.*
Ann.

It was ironic that she should now be the one writing such
a letter and pleading for reconciliation. She would post it
immediately. Then she could only wait. Three weeks later,
still anxiously waiting, she received a warm letter from her
mother-in-law.

Bombay
8/6/80

Dear Ann,

*It is so good to hear that you want to come to us for
your holiday. Zal too is most pleased and says that
he can make all your travel arrangements through
a friend in London. Of course, you are very used to
managing all your own affairs but I believe that to do
this for you would ease his mind. He knows that he did
not always treat you well. He is a clever man but can
only show what he feels by organising such things for
us. This is how he will always be. My dear girl, you are
so clear-headed and honest. It was hard for us when
Sam married you but we were wrong to have had any
thought that this was a big mistake. He was very right
to follow his heart. If we all had loving hearts and
followed them, how much better things would be and
how much of suffering we would all be spared. It is good
that after these difficulties you still want to come back
to us. There is always a place for you here with us. You
also will meet Cyrus's children, your niece, Gulshan,*

and your nephew, Darius. Such things are important. They are sweet children. You may feel some heartache when you see the little boy. He is very like our dear Sam. Both Cyrus and his wife, Mehru, work and are always very busy. I have the children here with me very often and we four can have some happy times together. Zal will now write to you about your travel plans and I will start to think of getting things ready to welcome you. You have been away far too long.

Perin.

Two days later, there was a second airmail letter on the mat. She read the sender's name, Mrs F.Panday. Afraid to read it straight away, she carried it through into the kitchen and, her heart beating fast, sat down at the table. Then, drawing a deep breath, she opened it.

Delhi
10/6/80

Dear Ann,

Well! I had always expected to hear that you had realised your mistake in running away from us but I had not thought to have to wait so long. I was, of course, extremely angry with you for throwing away what I believed was your second chance at real happiness with Hari, but I admit that I was much taken with him and may well have let my own feelings prejudice me. I still see your behaviour towards him as uncharacteristically callous and on this I will never change my mind but I do now understand what was driving you. My dear girl, don't think that you have to ask me for forgiveness. I know, who better, having been with you on that dreadful day when we heard about Sam, just what you have been made to suffer. I am only too delighted and relieved to hear that, after so much pain and all your unrelenting efforts to rebuild your life, you are at last finding some way of dealing with all your problems and dilemmas. I agree that you must stay in England. I admire you for all you have achieved there. You are, as always, finally realistic, whatever emotions have torn you apart. I also agree that you need to return to India and to us. It may be a little hard to get back immediately to the ease we used to feel, such a long time apart will have an effect but, whatever has happened, we are your friends and we are anxious to have you with us again. Now let us get down to practicalities. When are you coming? How long will you stay with Zal and Perin and when are you likely to come to us? How long......

Ann could not read anymore there were tears in her eyes. She wiped them away on her sleeve and, looking out of the window, saw, not her much loved Norfolk garden, but a wide verandah in Delhi where she had once sat weeping for Sam.

Also by Joan Khurody
No-one Mentioned Bandits

"This is the amazing experience of an English woman in a strange land. A perceptive and sensitive description of a moment in Indian history, beautifully written. Well worth a read."

Amazon reader review – 5 stars S. Lister 29/7/15

"I usually have two or three books to read at all times, choosing which to read at any time according to my mood. However, since buying this fascinating and beautifully written book, it's the only one. It's an extraordinary story, all the more so because it's true. It's full of colourful characters, textures and tastes. Joan's modestly stated courage shines through it all. A wonderful summer read."

Amazon reader review – 5 stars P. Wise 10/7/15

"This is a very well written and fascinating account of the love story of a young English girl and an Indian in the 1950s and her courage in leaving her home to marry him and live in a remote part of Northern India, not knowing what lay ahead. The heat, colour and cultures and the people of India are all brought vividly to life. Thoroughly recommended."

Amazon reader review – 5 stars Mrs C. 28/7/15

"A wonderfully emotive story. Beautifully written and keeps you enthralled until the end. I read this on holiday and couldn't put it down. The story resonates all the more because it's true."

Amazon reader review – 5 stars Debbie R. 13/10/15

"A recently read this book and enjoyed it very much. It is well written and easy to read. Once you begin, you will find it hard to put it down. It gives a good insight into life in England and India in the 1950s and 60s and the problems faced by those challenging the rigid regimes of the day, when mixed marriages were frowned upon. The descriptive passages of life for a young girl in rural India are great and paint a very vivid picture. If like me, you remember life in that period you will be transported back to those days and appreciate the courage of those who dared to break the mould. For a young person reading the book in today's fast and multicultural society, it will open a window into a new world. Well worth a read, folks."

Goodreads reader review – 4 stars   M. Buzzard 15/10/15

Contact www.ypdbooks.com or
see author's website www.joankhurody.co.uk